# THE KILLER IN US

## A Novel of Reckoning

Ted Taber

# ACKNOWLEDGEMENTS

I couldn't have attempted an undertaking of this magnitude without the support and patience of my wonderful wife, Sandy. She was my partner in the long and late hours of editing, re-editing, re-writing and organizing this manuscript from a raw idea to its completion. Her differing opinions on many fronts made difficult characters and complicated scenarios an easy read. I truly couldn't have done this without her expertise, ideas and unwavering support.

I must also extend my sincere thanks to Heather Valdovinos for her help in character development, Jim Abeltin for sharing his courtroom expertise, Brandy Alvarado for our cover, Pat Williams for editing, and countless others for their input, research and suggestions.

A special thanks goes to author Ron von Freymann for his unabashed critiques, direction and encouragement, and for inspiring me to produce this work of fiction.

# 1

Donny Blackmon was a bully who would make any bully proud. He was not the biggest boy in our fourth grade class in the small town of Carpelton, Michigan, in fact he wasn't really big at all, but he was tough and scrappy and always spoiling for a fight. Like most bullies, he relentlessly sought out weaker victims to pick on, and never missed an opportunity to brutally beat the hell out of anyone he thought was an easy target. The premise was that he wanted their milk money, but there was more to it than that.

Donny liked to hurt people.

Some boys were afraid to fight back, thinking it was easier to surrender to a lesser beating than to resist, and be stomped worse for pissing Donny off. So they resigned themselves to a beating, cried all the way home and hoped for better days. I never surrendered in an effort to avoid more pain, but rather tried to find ways to placate Donny and perhaps divert his attention to something other than how much satisfaction he could get from hurting me.

I was born Christopher James, but my friends called me Chris. Some of the girls called me Chrissy. Donny Blackmon called me "Fuckface," a term from which he derived some peculiar satisfaction. Of course, the world was a different place compared to what it is today, and such language was not bantered around loosely. Because of the times and the innocence of my youth, I didn't know what a

"Fuckface" was. I did know that coming from Donny's lips, it sounded ominous, but I wasn't going to stop him in mid-pounding to ask for a definition. I thought I would find out sooner or later what it really meant, but for the time being, I tried to ignore it. I just correctly assumed it was meant to be bad.

It turned out, in later years, when some of his history became known, Donny had a violent drunk for a stepfather who liked to beat him every night for no apparent reason. Perhaps his stepfather simply abused him because he could, like Donny did with so many of the boys in school.

Compared to the pain Donny suffered from the angry blows of a grown man, the puny resistance a fourth grader could put up must have been laughable. Our punches were like powder-puffs in comparison to what he received daily, so when one of us fought back, the blows we landed on Donny had little or no effect.

After being knocked around a few times myself, I decided it was just easier to fork over the dime I had for milk money than to suffer the consequences. The problem was, it quickly became apparent the dime wasn't enough. What Donny really wanted and needed was to dominate, and he could only do that through the threats of violence that he could and would inflict. Every now and then, after he took our milk money, he beat up on us anyway.

It was a cool, crisp day in late fall, when I should have been thinking about the beauty of the changing leaves on the trees, that I decided this had to stop. The trouble was, there was only one way I could think of to end it, so I began making plans to kill Donny. Here I was, nine-years-old and planning a murder. It wasn't something I was proud of, but it was going to be necessary to ensure my own safety and the safety of others. And I needed to do it without being caught.

Even while planning it, I tried not to think of it as murder. I preferred to think of it as an act of survival, although I knew in my heart that was bullshit. I was afraid that at the rate Donny's need for dominance was escalating, he would one day kill me or some other boy, so I simply couldn't allow these beatings to continue.

I never knew for sure how many other boys Donny picked on, stole from, beat up or threatened and I really didn't care. I only cared about my own skin, but there was no one with whom to speak about it without consequences. I couldn't tell my sister, my parents or a teacher, for I knew if trouble found Donny because of me, there would be hell to pay. The other boys he bloodied probably felt the same way. He left no doubts about the measures he would take to punish anyone who crossed him.

As hard as I tried, my nine-year-old brain was incapable of formulating a successful, workable way to get rid of Donny without being caught. It was frightening in itself, but scarier yet was the thought of the repercussions if I attempted to kill him and failed. I was painfully young to be thinking about how to kill a classmate. It would be so much easier if he just moved away, but I knew that wasn't going to happen. Crime, especially murder, was not one of my childhood fantasies, so I didn't know where to begin.

Freedom eventually came, and when it did, it came purely and literally by accident. One late December afternoon, I was ice skating on the only pond in our town which was always flooded in winter for recreational use. In summer, one could probably call it a swamp, but in winter, when the water froze, it was a skate pond. We had not yet had the consistent sub-zero nighttime temperatures needed to be sure the ice was thick enough for skating, but being children, we thought bad things only happen to others. Disregarding all the warnings, we skated anyway, thin ice or not. The pond was around six to eight feet deep at its deepest and in other places there were mere inches of water to freeze for skating. A "No Skating" sign was always posted, most likely to release the town from any liability should someone drown.

On that cold, cloudy December day, about two dozen of us were skating on the questionably thin ice, getting the most out of our day. The penetrating westerly wind had a serious bite and the darkening sky held a promise of snow. I was happily skating alone at the far end of the pond, near the woods, trying to keep the wind at my back while working diligently at perfecting my best hockey moves. It was much more fun skating with the wind behind you, because you could reach exhilarating speeds with very little energy expended. When it became time to return, skating into the wind made it harder because for every three forward strides, it seemed like you were blown back two. The wind chill made it feel so cold it was almost paralyzing.

I was imagining going from end to end on a big rink in front of a huge crowd and scoring the winning goal, when I glanced over at a small grouping of trees in the middle of the pond. No longer sporting their summer leaves, they now starkly stood on a small island in the center. Much to my chagrin, there was Donny Blackmon skating my way. He must have spotted me and was coming to squeeze an extra dime out of me, or take whatever money I might be carrying. It was a safe bet that he was also coming over to hit me because he needed someone to hit.

I was alone at a remote side of the pond on a section where, because the flooding was so complete, the water created ice trails deep into the woods. The advantage for Donny and disadvantage for me was that we were completely isolated, so nobody would see him stealing from me or pounding on me. When I spotted him he was still quite far away, but I could imagine him salivating over his good fortune.

At the same moment I saw Donny, I heard a crackling under my skates, a sure indication that the ice was unsafe, and a warning that I should promptly get out of there. It briefly occurred to me how funny it would be if Donny crashed through the ice where it was so thin. I even had the fleeting thought that if he fell through the ice and I saved him, somehow it might exempt me from further bullying. For a short moment I fantasized about how grateful he would be if something bad happened and I was his rescuer. I immediately dismissed such a foolish thought. Donny? Grateful? Gratitude wasn't in Donny's vocabulary, so that would never happen.

When he came closer, hoping to avoid trouble, I casually called out, "Hey, Donny!"

Squinting beneath the brim of his filthy red hat, he focused on me through the ugly lids of those evil eyes and answered, "I'm gonna beat the shit outta you, Fuckface."

I knew at that moment there was never going to be a time when he would leave me alone. Neither of us could have known it then, but that threat sealed his fate.

As much to my surprise as his, I boldly retorted, "I don't think so, asshole."

Not used to being spoken to that way, Donny sputtered a few loud curses and surged ahead on the tips of his blades, trying to get a run at me. I brought my fists up defensively while backing away, to afford myself some time and distance before the inevitable fight.

He was about five feet away and closing fast when he let out a startled cry as the ice gave way beneath him. It seemed like it was all happening in slow motion as the sharp point of the blade on his right hockey skate broke through a patch of thin, clear ice. He quickly fell onto his knee, which crashed completely through, and opened a hole so big, the pond easily swallowed him.

The icy water must have been unbearably cold and for a moment I thought he was gone, but after an interminably long couple of seconds, he surfaced. He extended his icy, gloved hand to me in a grasping effort.

"Help me!" Donny pleaded through quivering lips.

I chanced a hurried look toward the other side of the pond and saw no one close enough to help or even see what was happening. For a moment, time stood still. He and I were the only two people on earth and I was the only person who could save Donny Blackmon.

At warp speed, my mind calculated the situation and my options. With a sudden wave of calmness, I made a fateful decision that changed my life forever.

I looked into his frightened eyes and quietly said, "Not today, Fuckface."

A fraction of a second later, he again slid below the surface. This time he didn't come back up.

With the decisive moment over, the eerie calm quickly evaporated and I frantically looked around again to see if anyone was watching. Seeing that there wasn't, I skated widely around the dangerously thin area as fast as my legs would go, to the snowbank at the edge of the other side of the pond, where my boots faithfully waited under a broken green bench. I pulled warm, dry socks from my inside coat pocket, changed out of my skates and walked the half mile home on shaky legs.

It was so unexpected and fast, I couldn't begin to process all that had happened until I was well on my way home. I wasn't sure my legs were going to hold up, but they did. I needed to pull myself together, before someone noticed the shaking going on inside me. I made it home, seemingly more in control than I actually was and somehow managed to appear calm in front of my parents. Not that they would have noticed.

Donny was reported missing by his mother at about 11PM, when he hadn't come home from skating. She wasn't alarmed sooner because it was not unusual for him to come in well after curfew. He often stayed out late, hoping his stepfather was in bed sleeping, so he might avoid a beating.

They recovered Donny's body the next day. The fire rescue crew who found him speculated that when he broke through and went beneath the ice, he must have become disoriented and miscalculated where he entered the water. They theorized that he perhaps scrambled a few feet in the wrong direction and could not locate the hole he had fallen through. The Medical Examiner said he couldn't have lasted longer than a few seconds in water that cold.

Unable to pinpoint the exact time of his death, they questioned everyone who was on the pond that day. Some of the other skaters said they had seen him but there were no witnesses to him breaking through the ice. School officials and the Carpelton Police questioned all of us in a group and individually. When they came to me, I said I had been there skating, but that I didn't recall seeing Donny at all. I repeated the same story to my parents and stuck to it.

The school lowered the flag to half-staff and the town mourned the untimely death of this poor little boy.

The day they conducted his funeral, school was closed so everyone could attend, but I didn't go, for obvious reasons. I wondered how many others in my class also stayed away from the service. Donny, quite frankly, had almost no friends.

It's easy to look back and speculate on how different things might have been, had I been thinking like an adult instead of an inexperienced child and how the confrontation with Donny could have been different. But I wasn't thinking like an adult, the confrontation didn't happen differently and it was what it was. The end result was, because Donny fell through the ice and drowned, I had milk money every day without Donny beating me up just because he could. I figured there were more than a few other boys getting proper nourishment as well, now that Donny Blackmon was gone. The scariest thing about the whole incident for me was the revelation that maybe deep down inside, there's a killer lurking in everyone. We just don't know it until the killer in us is called upon to act.

I was elated that I had faced a very dangerous situation, done what I had to do and lived through it.

Life was good. For now.

# 2

Fourth grade became fifth, then sixth, and as I grew into puberty, I often asked myself if any of that business with Donny really happened. It was quite a nightmare, and being so young and innocent when it all went down, sometimes it seemed like it must have just been a bad dream. Of course I knew it wasn't, but a child's mind can't absorb something of that magnitude without haunting questions. Perhaps I wished it had been someone else who let Donny drown, but wishing wasn't changing anything. Somebody had to do it and fate simply chose me that day. I told myself it wasn't my fault and that some people just need killing. I didn't blame myself for not trying to help Donny Blackmon because he was a beast of prey. Even at the tender age of nine, I knew no good would have come from trying to save him. If there was a crime here at all, it was a nine-year-old being placed in such a life-altering situation. I made myself put any guilt I was feeling out of my head.

Donny's death was not mourned by many of his peers because of the bully he was and it's likewise doubtful any of the teachers missed his troublemaking. The evil that Donny was had been a dark time for me, and who knew how many others. I was confident that my life was blessed without him and I looked forward to getting on with it like a normal boy.

I was a God-fearing young man, attending Sunday school regularly, but I never really thought I had committed a sin. All I did was let a monster die before he killed somebody. Chances were, I probably couldn't have saved Donny even if I had tried. More than likely, I would have just drowned with him.

I sometimes wondered what I would have done if I'd been Catholic and had to go to confession. I was really happy I wasn't Catholic.

In sixth grade, I found a new girlfriend. This was nothing new for me because although I was gangly and painfully thin, I was also cute, so there were many girls who were attracted to me.

My latest girlfriend, Wendy Farmer, was blonde, petite and shy, and I liked her very much. She had been in another class for the first five years, so although I occasionally saw her on the playground, I never got to know her. Using the word "petite" to describe her might be just a kind description to use, because the truth of the matter was that she was skinny, just like me. She lived at the lower end of a cul-de-sac in a housing tract on the banks of the St. Joseph River at the north end of town, about a mile away. That distance doesn't sound like much, but we seldom left our immediate neighborhoods because that's where our friends lived. We were too young to drive, so I never saw Wendy away from school.

We were very attracted to each other, smiling, winking and flirting with each other in class all day but strangely, on the playground, she played hard to get. That was alright because I really didn't want to take any teasing from the other kids about having a girlfriend. And I knew I couldn't live with the chant of "Chrissy and Wendy sitting in a tree…" and all the other taunting childhood songs, so it was good for me to keep my infatuation to myself. Once I was older, it would be another story. I was just a kid, so why would I want to advertise that I had a crush on a girl?

When seventh grade came around and we were now in Junior High, Wendy and I were still in the same classes and still had a mutual attraction. We began going to the Junior High School dances, called "Socials," where the boys stood on one side of the gym, punching each other on the arm and nervously horsing around, while music played to an almost empty dance floor. The girls congregated on the other side, shyly looking over at the boys. The exceptions were the few girls who went out on the floor and danced with another girl.

I never understood why boys would pay hard-found money to go to these socials and then just stand there with the guys. I went there to dance, not to act like a goofball with my stupid friends. As soon as I arrived on that first dance night, I went directly over and asked Wendy to dance. We were the only boy/girl couple on the floor. She wore a pink dress with a white sweater and I remember wearing my favorite red jacket.

We were oblivious to all that was going on around us, and we put on a show. It was one of those great times a teenager never forgets.

After going to a few of these socials, Wendy's mother finally let her go to a movie with me. It was our first date without a chaperone. That Saturday afternoon we took the bus to the city and saw a funny movie starring Jimmy Durante. The name of the movie escapes me now, but if I close my eyes, I can almost smell the wisp of perfume Wendy wore that day. We laughed at the silliness of the movie, popcorn was cheap, soda was cheaper and I was wishing the afternoon would go on forever. Like all things, good and bad, the movie ended and we had to find another place to see each other. The library provided us with just the place.

After a couple of chance meetings at the library, I finally saw an opportunity and while flirting at the door, I kissed her. When I did, she cried, "I can't!" To my surprise, she ran away, leaving me outside on the back step of the library with an armful of books checked out to her. Completely confused, I stood there like a dope, trying to figure out what I did that could have been so wrong.

At first I thought she was playing hard to get again, but when she didn't come back, I had little choice but to carry the books down the long hill to her small, yellow house. I rang the doorbell, expecting

Wendy to laughingly open it and tell me it was a joke, but the door was opened by her father. He was unshaven, wearing a soiled tee shirt, jeans and brown sandals on very dirty feet. He asked what I wanted. I identified myself and told him I had some books for Wendy that she had checked out at the library.

He roughly asked, "So why do you have them?"

When I tried to explain that she left the library without them, he said, "Wendy isn't allowed to have boyfriends, so just give them to me and stay away from here."

I gave him the books and without another word, he closed the door in my face. Trekking back up that long hill to go home, it felt like my shoes were filled with cement. As if that wasn't bad enough, two big dogs chased me until they tired of it and went after something more fun. Then it started to rain. It wasn't a very good day.

I couldn't understand why Wendy ran away like she did and why her father was so upset with me for bringing the books to her. I didn't think I had done anything wrong and I hoped we could straighten things out when I saw her in school.

It turned out to be just the opposite. When I saw Wendy the next day, she ignored me in class, and then went out of her way to avoid me at lunch. I was clearly confused. It was just a kiss!

After two days of heartbreak, I decided that I could play that game too. I went back to goofing around with my dopey friends, punching each other on the arm, taunting "flinch!" and all of the things boys do, but I wasn't getting much satisfaction from hanging out with the guys. They may have been my buddies, but they weren't helping me get my mind off Wendy.

About a week later, Wendy and I again began giving each other the long looks in class. I thought perhaps we were on the mend from whatever it was that had happened. I couldn't imagine that trying to kiss her was such a big deal, and I wondered if she thought I was being too forward. I was only a seventh grader, so I still had a lot to learn about girls.

We had term papers due before long, so we soon met at the library again. I moved over to sit next to her and despite getting dirty looks and being shushed by the old lady Librarian a couple of times, I talked with Wendy and expressed my desire to see her alone.

I asked, "What happened that day on the library steps? I thought you liked me!"

She replied, "I do like you, Christopher, but it's complicated. My father won't let me be with boys. He would kill me and my mother too if he found out she let me go to the dance socials, let alone to a movie with you."

I said, "But I just want to be with you!"

She quickly answered, "Me too!"

I asked her to meet me outside, and before she could reply, I got up and went out to the back stoop of the library, where no one could see us from the street. I waited, and about five minutes later, she came out. She didn't say a word, but walked up and kissed me, right on the mouth. She kissed me with a passion far beyond any kiss from my experience. It made me a bit lightheaded and although she couldn't know it, I was more than a little embarrassed. I was afraid my lack of experience was showing. If it was, she never let on.

After the kiss, she blushed and said, "My father would kill me if he knew I did that."

I couldn't understand what the power was that her father had over her that caused such fear, but I quickly put it out of my head. I kissed her again, with all the fervor this 13-year-old boy could muster. It was the first big-time kiss of my life.

Then she broke away and said, "I've got to go." Off she went and once again I found myself standing at the back of the library, only this time I had a warm feeling all over. The shoes that felt like cement the other day were now walking on air.

As often as we could, we met at the library and slipped out the back door to make out like they did in the movies. As the weather became warmer, with spring approaching fast, we began meeting in the cemetery behind the library where there was no chance of anyone seeing us. Sometimes we made out and sometimes we just talked. I liked to talk, but I liked making out better.

Wendy was easy to converse with, but she often made me feel like there was a barrier between us that I couldn't breach. It kept us at a distance from each other despite the tentative intimacies we shared. Sometimes it was hard to keep track of her serious and playful moods, but as long as she liked me, I decided not to worry too much about it.

Then one day in the cemetery, while kissing her, I made the mistake of sliding my hand under her sweater and cupping her little breast. She jumped like my hand was on fire and started to cry. She said she could never do that and that if her father caught me touching her like that he would kill us both. I asked, "How could your father know unless someone told him? He wouldn't find us here even if he came looking!"

She replied, "He always knows where I am and if I do something wrong he swears he will kill me."

When I asked what made her think he could do that, she replied in a frightened voice, "You don't know my father. He says he always knows. And I believe him."

After a while she calmed down and we kissed some more. Before we parted, she allowed me to briefly cup her budding breast again, but she was doing it because I wanted to, not because she did.

I was getting an inkling that everything might not be as it should be. Wendy was far too afraid of her father; much more than the average kid is afraid of their parent. She often spoke of her desire to get away and never come back. I was beginning to find it odd that she was often talking about running away. She seemed to be trying to find a way to escape from something and every time we strayed from just kissing, she would again go back to her fear of her father and his control.

I dwelled on it for a while and maybe wouldn't have been so suspicious about the goings on there if I hadn't seen the movie "Johnny Belinda." It was about a girl who was being molested. I don't remember much about the movie now, except that I think it was Jane Wyman who played the role of the girl who was violated. It made me wonder if maybe something was going on in the Farmer house that wasn't quite right. I couldn't imagine that anyone would molest their own child, but I supposed it did happen. I just wasn't prepared to think it was happening to Wendy.

# 3

Wendy told me her father, Leonard, was a chronic drinker, who favored his own homemade brew. He no longer worked, although he must have at some time. They were supported by whatever form of Welfare there was in those days. She said he had a history of diabetes and heart trouble and probably couldn't hold a job if he wanted to. He grew his own grapes and made his own wine because he couldn't afford to buy it. At that time, many neighboring people had grape arbors. Before I found out about Mr. Farmer making wine from his own grapes, I had always wondered why grapes were so popular in my neighborhood. I thought people just ate a lot of grapes or used them to make jelly.

I didn't see Mr. Farmer often, but most of the times I did, he was unstable and obviously drunk. I didn't know how he could function normally, being that way all the time, but I never brought it up to Wendy. As young as I was, I didn't know much about diabetes, but I was almost sure that if you had the disease, you were not supposed to drink alcohol or eat sweets.

Watching Wendy's reactions to the awkward advances of this inexperienced teenaged boy when we were together made me wonder what was so bad about what we did. She would enjoy touching sometimes and other times she would be almost shaking with fear. And at no time would she ever let me see any of her body that she thought was forbidden. Even the untrained eye of a teenage boy could pick up on her strange behavior. At that age I expected her to be as curious as me, but her curiosity was always upstaged by fear.

One Saturday afternoon Wendy had a birthday party and her parents allowed her to invite a couple of boys as well as the handful of girlfriends she had. Naturally, I was one of the boys invited. We played some games outdoors and one was a game similar to Hide and Seek. I was avoiding capture by hiding behind their house, hugging one wall right near a window. I heard her parents talking in what sounded like a disagreement. It escalated quickly, voices were raised and I heard her mother say, "I know you're fiddling with that girl! I can see it in her face, and I'm not going to let you get away with it! Either it stops now or I'm going to the police!"

Her father answered hotly, "What I do with my kid is my business and if you tell anyone, so help me I'll kill you!"

I ran from my hiding place before I was discovered and quickly found a new hiding place where I could take a minute to think about what I just heard. Evidently, my suspicions were right.

That tore it. Leonard Farmer had to go.

I left the party shortly after that, wrestling all the way home over how unfair and cruel the world is. I questioned why nature doesn't stop producing these monsters and spare innocent people harm and death. What a better world it would have been if Adolph Hitler's mother had miscarried or if John Wilkes Booth's mother had not borne a healthy son.

Throughout the history of the world, there has always been an abundance of evil people who had no business breathing the precious oxygen we share.

I decided then and there, I was going to see to it that Leonard Farmer stopped molesting his daughter. Now the question was, how?

Wendy and I were just average kids with raging hormones, and what we did was considered normal by most everyone's standards. We were very young and weren't anywhere close to having intercourse. We were just kids experimenting with something new and exciting.

We had urges, but at this point neither of us was ready to try anything beyond a little petting and making out. For me, even this was pretty heavy stuff and I enjoyed every minute of my time with Wendy, but I knew the dangers of going any further. Being so young, I was too unsure of myself to press for anything else, so finding out now that Wendy had been and was maybe still being molested by her father was a shock. It was more than I was going to stand for, and I coldly decided the sand was rapidly running out of Leonard Farmer's hourglass.

# 4

**W**endy told me many times that her father was cruel to both her and her mom, and from what I had observed, I never doubted it. Now I knew for sure. My mind was awash with visions of what I wanted to do and how I would do it. I had thoughts jumping all over the place, from wishing he would get hit by a bus, to hoping that he would drink himself to death.

Because of the sheer horror of what he was doing, and my building anger, it seemed quite natural to make the decision to kill Wendy's father. It shouldn't be that hard, should it? I couldn't expect to get him out on the pond on thin ice, so I had to think of another way. I knew that Donny's death had been a series of extremely fortunate events and had the ice not broken, that day could have produced a very different outcome. It probably wouldn't have been very nice for me. If I was going to do something like that again, I was going to have to be a lot smarter. He might be a drunk, but Mr. Farmer was still an adult, so if I was going to do something this drastic, I had to make myself think like an adult in order to succeed.

I remembered a time when I was a few years younger, visiting my grandfather, that I learned an almost forgotten lesson about something he had to do to protect his chickens from predators. My grandfather always had a variety of chickens, ducks, pigeons and a smattering of other livestock, but he was mostly a bird fancier. One time when I was visiting, he had just finished burning the carcasses of a dozen or more of his birds, because some dogs jumped the three-foot fence surrounding the chicken yard and killed them. They didn't eat them, but simply killed them for sport. I had never thought about dogs, raccoons or other predators getting into the chicken yards or into the henhouses, but then, I was just a kid and completely clueless about the need to protect one's livestock. I always thought the fence was just for keeping the chickens inside the yard.

After disposing of the dead chickens and mending the broken fence, my grandfather confided that he knew a way to get rid of the dogs without anyone knowing how it happened. He placed a half-dozen metal feed cans around the outside perimeter of the chicken yard, partially filled them with dog food and added a little bit of what could pass for gravy. Then he poured a cap-full of radiator antifreeze into the mix. He said it only took a few ounces to kill a good sized dog once they ate or drank it and that it was the only way to keep his chickens safe, short of shooting the dogs. He said the neighbors would raise Cain if he just shot them, and it was probably against the law to kill them anyway, even to protect his birds.

He said antifreeze has a sweet taste that animals like, so the dogs wouldn't hesitate to eat the food. I never asked about it afterward, but it must have worked because I never heard any new stories about dogs killing his chickens. Thinking back, I never saw any dogs around his chicken yard again either.

Recalling that remedy for my grandfather's killer dog problem gave me the idea of using automobile antifreeze to get rid of a two-legged predator I knew. I never doubted that I had the nerve to poison Leonard Farmer, I just had to find a way to do it without it being traced back to me. After a week of mulling over possible scenarios, I decided that it could be done but it would take some good planning and a little luck. The hardest part was figuring out a way to get Wendy's father to drink it. I couldn't expect to just hand Mr. Farmer a glass of antifreeze and say "Bottoms up!"

One day, playing in Wendy's back yard, with her father already so drunk that we knew he couldn't come to the window to see I was there, it began to rain. Pent-up energy in the purple sky violently unleashed searing bolts of lightning, furious thunder and rain that came down in huge, soaking drops. We ran into an old wooden shed near the stone wall on the north side of their yard to get out of the downpour. It was a good sized shed, about ten feet wide and twenty feet long, with wood floors, and tarpaper on the roof and sides to keep the rain and wind out. There were split-paned windows on two sides and a door at each end. Whoever built it must have been good with tools because although it was obviously home-made, it was quite sturdy. There were carpentry tools of all kinds neatly hanging on pegboards, and dozens of pieces of broken down old furniture that looked like something someone had at one time been restoring. All of those tools and broken furniture made me wonder if before Mr. Farmer began drinking himself stupid, he had a talent for restoration of antique furniture and some other wood-working abilities.

Another wall of the shed was lined with three rows of wooden shelves holding about forty bottles with corks in the tops. When I asked Wendy what was in all those bottles, she said that was her daddy's wine. She said he drank two or three bottles of the wine every day, unless he passed out before he finished the last bottle. They were lined up in the order that they would be consumed. The bottles nearest the door toward the house were todays or tomorrows, with the ones beside them being the next days' bottles and so on. Evidently, he was occasionally sober enough to make up a batch of his homemade hooch, with his dutiful wife placing the bottles on the shelves in the order they were made.

His stock was continually being rotated so he drank the oldest first. I thought it ironic that a drunken slob like Mr. Farmer could still have the where-with-all to keep his booze that well organized. I guessed life was a matter of priorities.

I saw opportunity in the shed that day, so I began to formulate my plan. Remembering my grandfather's words that it took only a couple of ounces of anti-freeze to finish off a healthy dog, I thought about twice that dosage should do the job for a piece of shit like Leonard Farmer. I knew antifreeze was made to mix with water, so I had no doubt it would blend well with wine. My plan was beginning to take an exciting turn.

My dad kept a couple gallons of anti-freeze in the cellar on his chemical shelf along with a can of brake fluid, a tub of multi-use grease and a couple quarts of 30W non-detergent motor oil. I guess he used all of these in his old car, although I had never seen him use any of them. I didn't think he knew how to lift the hood, let alone do a repair. He was one of the least mechanical men I ever knew. Give him two pieces of wood, a box of nails and a hammer and he could build you a house, but don't ask him to check your oil.

I started looking for a way to use some of that antifreeze without it being obvious that it was gone. To lug a gallon over to Wendy's would not only be too cumbersome, it was far more than I needed for what I was planning. It was about a mile to the Farmer's house from mine, using the fields and paths through the woods, following the St. Joseph River. That would be my route, both to and from, if I was going to do this. It was imperative for no one to see me coming or going. I didn't need to be implicated in anything suspicious, especially after what had happened to Donny Blackmon. Bumblers they may be, but even small town cops can occasionally get lucky and put two and two together. Especially when there are too many accidents.

I needed to get into Mr. Farmer's shed, pop a few corks, dump a little bit of wine out of a half dozen bottles and top them off with anti-freeze. The best I could do was guess how many doses it might take because this was all new to me. I didn't want to just make him sick, and I didn't want to have a bunch of wine bottles left in the shed with anti-freeze in them. I did have a distant cousin who was a doctor, but I could hardly ask him to advise me on the dosage.

I found an old glass Bluing bottle, the size and shape of a small hot water bottle which didn't seem too large for the task at hand. I tucked it up under my shirt and looked in a mirror to see how noticeable it was. It looked like I was carrying a small animal there, so I quickly gave up on that idea. If someone saw me with a bottle bulging under my shirt or coat and Mr. Farmer turned up dead from poisoning, it wouldn't take too long for someone to wonder if there was a connection. I tossed that idea out the window and threw the bottle in the trash. Whatever I used to carry the antifreeze would have to be just the right size and shape to ensure success. I wasn't going to settle for something that might be just good enough. It wouldn't be wise to have to make two trips, so it had to be big enough to carry what I needed yet small enough that carrying it would not be remembered, should someone see me. I hoped to avoid that, but one can never be sure and I wanted to have all the possibilities covered.

Then one day, visiting my uncle's farm in the next town, while tinkering with some of the harvesting equipment and tractors he had parked under a lean-to, I came across a small metal flask which he probably used from time to time to sneak a swallow or two. I guess he must have needed an occasional belt of firewater while working in the fields. The flask appeared to be just the ticket for carrying a small amount of liquid without being detected. I thought it would be ironic that something designed for discretely hiding booze was going to be the tool used to kill off Mr. Farmer, whose entire life revolved around booze. Tucked in the back pocket of my jeans, it wasn't even visible unless you were really looking. It wouldn't be detectable and unless someone bumped into me there would be no way to know I was carrying it. I didn't plan to get that close to anyone, so I thought I had finally found the items I needed to pull this off.

In the meantime, I saw Wendy almost every day during the summer, always with an eye on that shed. We still managed to occasionally find a place where we were unobserved, so we could keep our youthful passions alive.

School resumed, with autumn in the air, leaves rapidly changing color as they neared the end of their cycle, and dusk coming earlier every day. One Friday night when darkness was falling after a wildly red autumn sunset, it was soon time for Wendy to go into the house and for me to go home. Before she did, she went to their shed and grabbed a bottle off the first shelf to take in with her. She said she would catch hell from her father if she came in empty handed.

I walked home on the roads connecting our streets, but before I went in, I skirted down the bike path beside our house and went into the cellar. I retrieved the flask I had hidden so well in a space above a big weight-bearing support beam under the floor, and quickly took the cap off of a half empty gallon of anti-freeze. Using a battered metal funnel to avoid spillage, I filled the flask about two thirds full, recapping the jug and the flask. I didn't think my father would ever notice any of the antifreeze was missing. I didn't think he ever had cause to use it. I quickly dismissed the idea of putting some water in to fill the jug back up. My father didn't notice things like that, so I knew I was safe.

I grabbed some old work gloves from under the tool bench in the corner, left the cellar and tossed the flask and the gloves into some tall grass at the base of a rotting elm tree beside the bike path. I knew they wouldn't be seen in the grass. Then I went into the house for supper.

After eating, I spent the evening watching some television and listening to my father telling stories from his childhood, while my mother slaved over an ironing board. Finally, it was time to go to sleep. I went up the stairs and quickly climbed into bed. Except for my shoes, I kept my clothes on. My sister was my only sibling and we had our own bedrooms so no one could see that I was still dressed.

Tonight was the night.

# 5

While my parents were downstairs, engrossed in an episode of "I Love Lucy," I was in bed finalizing the plan for how I was going to kill Leonard Farmer. I tried to visualize myself going over there, doing the deed and hot-footing it home without being discovered. I was new at this and scared to death. Wanting to cover all the bases in my mind, I tried to think of anything I could have forgotten. I walked myself through it over and over, trying to imagine anything that could go wrong and how I would deal with it if it did. I waited until a little after midnight, when everyone had finally gone to sleep. With my heart thumping loudly in my chest, I put my shoes on and stepped out my bedroom window onto the roof of the back porch. I carefully edged over and climbed down a trellis on the side of the house which was now sparsely covered with ivy. There was barely a moon, so I didn't think I would be seen, but I still waited a few minutes, keeping perfectly still before I made a dash to the base of the rotting elm tree. I retrieved my gloves and the flask of antifreeze from the tall grass beside the tree and ran off through the field on the banks of the river, north toward Wendy's house.

Wendy lived over a mile away, but I ran through knee-high grass, rocks, dirt and sand along the base of that long hill beside the river in just the little light supplied by the moon. I was dodging rocks and jumping over driftwood like a cross country runner. When I finally approached her house, I stopped for a moment to listen. All was quiet except for a clanging in my ears which I finally recognized as my own heartbeat.

The Farmers had no neighbors close enough to be spying, but to be sure, I crouched down, making myself as small as possible. I scrambled silently, but as fast as I could to the back of the shed, exercising great care to approach from a direction where I couldn't be seen from the house. I donned my gloves, so I would leave no fingerprints, not remembering that as often as I had been there with Wendy, my prints must already be all over the place. After a long minute I worked up the courage to open the latch and soundlessly slide in past the old wooden door.

I was in!

There was a street light a short distance away that shone just enough into the high windows on the street side of the shed, so I wouldn't need a flashlight. It was a good thing, because I had forgotten to bring one. I didn't remember to bring a damn flashlight! It scared me almost to distraction to have planned so carefully and come all this way, making such elaborate preparations, and then forgot to bring something as simple as a flashlight. Some operator I was!

What I needed was courage and determination and instead, despite the coolness of the fall night air, I was sweating like a hooker at High Mass. What if I had overlooked or forgotten some other important thing that could bring this crashing down around me? Suppose I opened the door and came face to face with Wendy, coming out to get her father another bottle, or Mrs. Farmer running the same errand, or, God forbid, the old man himself? Those fears almost made me run out of there and forget this crazy idea, but remembering the look on Wendy's face when she mentioned the fear of her father made me stay the course.

After painstakingly closing the door behind me, I held my breath for what seemed like an hour. When I was sure I was alone and undetected, I took four bottles down from the first shelf. I carefully twisted out the corks so I wouldn't break them, and poured what I judged to be a couple ounces of wine from each of them into the pots of some young geranium plants Wendy's mother was protecting from an early frost. Then I filled the bottles back up with anti-freeze from the flask. I firmly replaced the corks in the bottles, gently turned them upside down and back a few times to completely mix the antifreeze with the wine, and returned them to the shelf in the exact order from which I had taken them. My hands were sweating in my gloves, but I kept them on for the entire time, still fearful of leaving fingerprints.

In retrospect, the chore I had envisioned taking a half hour only took about six minutes, but because of the seriousness of what I was doing, and the fear of being discovered, it seemed like it was taking forever. I thought for sure it would be noon tomorrow and I would still be there.

When I finished and everything was back where it belonged without a drop being spilled, I retrieved my flask and carefully let myself out of the shed. It took all the will power I could muster to remain still for a few minutes and make sure I hadn't been detected. When I was sure, I flew on winged feet as fast as I could run to get away from there.

Halfway home, by the river's edge, I unscrewed the cap from the flask and flung them both into the river as far as I could, followed by my work gloves. I cautiously approached my house, quickly climbed the trellis and entered my room through the unlocked window, quietly took off my clothes and slid under the covers. I laid there for the rest of the night, trembling from the rush of actually pulling it off. Confident no one had seen me, all I could do now was wait

# 6

It was a painfully long weekend, wondering if anything had happened. It had been a huge decision for someone as young as me to premeditate and carry out a plan like that, and no small feat to purposely kill a person even though you know they are pure evil.

As the weekend wore on with no news coming from my parents, television or newspaper, I wondered if it had all been for nothing. Communication was not the best in our small town, although I'm sure there was a grapevine to which children were not privy. I began wondering if I was going to have to come up with another plan.

Finally it was Monday morning and I was afraid to go to school. All I could think was that Wendy would come in and tell me her father had suffered from a stomach ache all weekend, but with the help of Pepto Bismol, had come through it. Even worse would have been Wendy coming in and saying they discovered someone had put antifreeze in her father's wine, or that her mother drank the wine and died. I hadn't thought of that before. It almost took more guts to go to school that day than it had taken to implement the plan to poison Leonard Farmer.

When I arrived at school, I looked for Wendy, but she appeared to be late. Then I really started to get nervous. Had my plan actually worked?

After a while, the teacher came in to greet us and announced that because of an unexpected death in her family, Wendy Farmer would not be at school today. She encouraged us all to say a prayer for Wendy and her mother, and for the soul of her father, and to ask for Divine help in making it through this bad time. She gave no other details and I wasn't going to ask.

I didn't know how I should feel, but one immediate feeling was relief. Relief that the antifreeze evidently worked, relief that Wendy and her mother could have a decent life without that monster in their house and relief that Wendy and I would be able to do whatever we wanted to do without living in constant fear of her father. I was guardedly euphoric. Trying to be focused at all in school that day was a total loss, but it raised no eyebrows because we were all preoccupied with this event. The rest of the class didn't know that my preoccupation was very different from theirs.

I felt no guilt, because I considered Mr. Farmer no better than Donny Blackmon. In fact, I thought he was worse, doing what I was so sure he had been doing. He was someone without whom the world would be a better place. For sure, Wendy would be better off. I knew I had done the right thing.

Strangely enough, there wasn't a big flap over Mr. Farmer's death. Oh, the busybodies were cackling over their back fences, to be sure, but there was no outcry of any kind to find out why he died, nor was anything mentioned about his welfare status or drinking habits. It all seemed to be kept pretty hush-hush.

The end result was that Leonard Farmer's death was ruled as Accidental Alcohol Poisoning, undoubtedly because everyone, including the town officials, knew he was a chronic drunk. No autopsy was performed because of his history and old Leonard was laid to rest as just another drunken loser who died too young. If there had been a Temperance League, there probably would have been parades pointing out the evils of alcohol, but in this small town there were many closet drinkers, both men and women. Perhaps it would have been too hypocritical for anyone to outwardly condemn his passing from the sin of drinking.

What I had not anticipated was that Wendy's mom had no close relatives nearby and because her husband was the man he was, they were left penniless. They did not own their property, but were just renters, so having no money except for what welfare would provide for two of them and having to pay funeral expenses, they were destitute. Wendy and her mom immediately moved to her sister's home in Maine.

Well, that was a heck of a note!

I was very upset that the mission I so painstakingly carried out to make my life with Wendy that much better had completely backfired. I hadn't taken into consideration anything like this happening and there wasn't a thing I could do about it.

Just that quickly, Wendy moved away and I never saw her again.

# 7

Time usually passes slowly in our youth but before I knew it, I was a freshman entering high school, and having more than my share of nervous anticipation over what it was going to be like. After the first week or two of being teased by the upperclassmen for being a rookie, the freshman hazing subsided and I looked forward to getting through high school and growing up as fast as I could. I knew even at that age, I was never going to be a lifetime student. So far, my childhood had been nothing to be nostalgic about and I wanted better times. Patience was not in my vocabulary, so I wanted to be done with school.

Just when I thought I was ready to get on to better times, I was saddled with a Home Room, Science, English, and Social Studies teacher named Mrs. Starchman. She was a beast. I never knew if she simply didn't like my looks or if there was something in my history or family that made her dislike me so, but from the very first day she treated me with open disdain.

Instead of welcoming me to her class, like she did with the other kids, she acted like I was shit on her shoes. Not knowing why this was happening made life in her class miserable.

From the beginning, she ridiculed my work, often pointing out to the entire class any mistakes I made or any incorrect answers I may have given. She used every opportunity to pick my work apart, and on more than one occasion mocked it when reading an essay or other effort of mine to the rest of the class. She said nasty, unprovoked things, like how judging by the way I put a paper together I was surely not going to be another Ernest Hemingway. That would be hurtful to any kid who thought they turned in good work.

When she did this, I could only sit there with my face beet-red, completely embarrassed, and take my lumps as she made my efforts look foolish. I'm sure she didn't realize what a mistake she was making in singling me out like that. I was somewhat of an expert at avenging wrongdoers, so little did she know, she was entering dangerous territory.

One day she was being particularly ornery with me, and I finally objected to her attitude. She gave me a heated tongue lashing, once again embarrassing me in front of the class. I responded by promising her and my classmates that someday I would piss on her grave. It may not have been the smartest thing I ever said but it stopped her short, while the class roared with delight. I, however, found myself in the guidance counselor's office with a note and a detention slip. He read the note, frowned deeply and lectured me on the perils of being a bad student. He explained in detail the wrong direction I was heading and where I would wind up if I didn't change my ways. It was the old "Wrong Side of the Tracks" and "Fork in the Road" lecture. I decided he must be a total idiot if he thought that a half-hour speech which he had obviously rehearsed well and practiced in front of a mirror would change my behavior and make me a better student for Mrs. Starchman. I looked petulant, however, and played the role of the repentant bad boy long enough to bullshit him. It worked quite well.

With his chest puffed out from a job well done, he proudly sent me back to class a changed boy.

At the same time, I took a job working after school and on Saturdays at a small, five-man manufacturing shop nearby which made many kinds of ceramic statues. Products ranged from very small figurines for knick-knacks to larger ones like birdbaths and jockeys for use as lawn ornaments. It was fun learning to mix plaster of paris cement in a huge vat, then pouring it into molds of different sizes and shapes for a variety of ornaments. I learned how to probe the mix with a slim-handled tool resembling a solid metal tube once the cement is poured into the big molds, to prevent air bubbles and to use other devices similar to wire hangers to get the same result for the small knick-knack ornaments. The object was to break up air bubbles before the mix hardened and dried, to ensure a smooth finish on the surface of the product.

This procedure popped the bubbles in the plaster while the mix was still mostly liquid. After it dried and was removed from the mold, and the rubber liner peeled off, any air holes left in the surface would have to be manually filled. It was a lot like how you would spackle nail holes in a plaster wall before painting. It amounted to using a small amount of the mix and applying it like putty to hand-fill the imperfections and smooth over the finish. The more air holes there were, the longer it took to produce a smooth surface. Naturally, the time spent doing this added to the cost of manufacturing. After the figurines were dried and hardened, we painted and sealed them, but we also occasionally sold them unpainted.

This was an interesting job for a teenager because there was always something different to do, rather than performing only one part of the manufacturing process over and over.

The fly in the ointment was our foreman, Kevin Cooper, who supervised me and the other five employees. He was a very strange man. I sensed something odd about him from my first day on the job, although initially he came off as a genuinely friendly and helpful guy.

He could be fun to work for and easy to get along with, but in a different sort of way. The initial creepy thing was how he seemed to take a special liking to me. The other four employees were adults, all grown men and I was the only teenager. I considered myself fortunate to work with them because they quickly accepted me as "The Kid." They liked to poke fun at me about girlfriends and things like that. I didn't mind because it was all so good natured, I felt like one of the guys. They talked openly about things I had never spoken about with adults before, like tits and ass, so I thought they were pretty cool, for grown-ups.

Unlike the four family guys there, the foreman, Kevin, was single and seemed to be more inclined to talk about sex than the older guys. I didn't see anything unusual about it, because I knew if I was among boys my own age, tits and ass would be the most common topic of discussion. Why wouldn't it be the same with grown men? All things considered, I thought it was a pretty good job.

In a short time, Kevin began offering me a chance to work overtime after the older guys went home. Business was booming and most of the time, at the end of the day there was still much to do.

Kevin taught me more and more about making these figurines and all of the steps and tricks which could be used in the manufacturing and finishing processes. For a while I thought it was a good opportunity to learn and was thankful that he was giving his time to tutor me.

Being a teenager in a small town, and never having experienced anything inappropriate directed at me, it took a while before I started to feel like Kevin was developing an interest that went beyond teaching me how to make plaster of paris figurines. His talk became more and more fixated on sex and sexual situations and I began to get uncomfortable when I thought he was getting too personal. It was all done under the guise of joking and bantering, like a "just-one-of-the-guys" thing, but there were quickly red flags popping up all over the place. The way he tried to make it all humorous and light-hearted put me in a place where showing I was uncomfortable would be insulting to him. The discomfort was still there, no matter how he tried to ignore it. Talking about tits and ass was one thing, but he was always pushing the envelope. Looking back, I think he was good at this.

I may have been young but I wasn't a total dope. I had heard of "Queers" and "Whores" and sex and knew a little bit about what went on in the world, but it still took a while for me to put two and two together and decide Kevin was a child molester.

It got so creepy that I started making excuses to leave when the older guys did, rather than work overtime, because I didn't want to be alone with this asshole. Then things would smooth over, Kevin would back off a little and I would let my guard down, wondering if it had all been my imagination.

Kevin began trying to worm information out of me to see how sexually active I was and what I knew and didn't know. I was fourteen, for crying out loud. How sexually active did he think I was?

Up until that time, I had experienced Wendy's kisses and her tiny breasts and whenever I had the chance, I enjoyed making out with her. Since Wendy moved away, there had been a few other girls my age whose hormones were starting to scream too, so an occasional make-out session or a quick feel of hot skin with a willing girl was a welcome adventure. Unfortunately, sexual escapades for this fourteen-year-old boy were not an everyday activity.

Kevin never let up trying to weasel details of every experience I ever had, and repeatedly told me how inexperienced I was for a boy of 14. It became a drag repeating who I had been with, and how far we had gone. At first it was fun because it felt like bragging, which is what teenaged boys do, but I quickly began to tire of it.

Then one day he asked me if I ever had any experiences with other boys. I initially thought he meant playing baseball or basketball or something, because what else could he mean?

When I finally understood where the talks with Kevin were going, I reached the limit of my personal discomfort in his presence. It began affecting me in other ways. I was beginning to have trouble sleeping, which affected my school work, my work at the factory and my play time. It's hard enough for a fourteen-year- old boy to deal with the new world of sex, without having an adult trying to lead you in a direction that's completely wrong for you. I wasn't interested in anything but girls and knew for sure that the perky tits and soft skin of the fairer sex excited me, yet here was an adult - my boss no less - who I was supposed to be able to trust, telling me I was wrong about myself.

Between the constant misinformation I was getting from Kevin and the relentless persecution at school from that Wildebeest, Mrs. Starchman, I was in quite a pickle. Kevin was enough of a problem, but add having a teacher in my face every minute of the school day, and it was almost more than this fourteen- year-old could stand. These were adults who I was supposed to learn from and trust, and they were tearing me apart.

Then Kevin started talking about touching and masturbation. If it wasn't before, it was now crystal clear where he was headed. I approached a couple of the older guys at work about him, but when I brought up the subject of Kevin saying things that didn't seem right, they laughed it off, saying he was just horsing around. I wanted them to take me seriously, but they never did. I couldn't talk with my parents about it either. Just thinking about that gave me the horrors.

I concluded Kevin was living proof of the difference between being a homosexual and being a predator. I began wondering how many boys he must have molested over the years. His demeanor was easy going and I could see where he might undermine a confused young boy, but he wasn't undermining me.

He was rapidly backing me into a corner, so to protect myself and the unknown number of teenaged boys he planned to conquer in years to come I decided Kevin had to go. I knew a wine guzzling pervert named Farmer he could consort with in another world and I was just the one to send him there.

# 8

It was Mrs. Starchman's good fortune that Kevin's advances were intolerable and much harder to deal with than her crusade against me, so I was going to put her ugly puss on the back burner for now. I couldn't take her and Kevin on at the same time, so her come-uppance would happen at a later date.

I was only a freshman in high school, but I was already beginning to fill out and was quite strong for my age, so I wasn't physically afraid of Kevin. I didn't like that he was backing me into a corner and forcing me into another killing, but I was convinced of his evil. If I tried to talk myself out of it, all I had to do was think about how many boys he already molested and how many more victims there could be if I didn't put a stop to it.

I had done this deed before, so I knew I could do it again, but I really wished I didn't have to. At the same time, I knew I had no choice. Kevin wasn't going away and his pressures were getting worse. He was barreling along like a runaway train. I had to do this for myself and for all the others whose innocence he had stolen.

I later discovered that many people being molested mistakenly think they're the only ones to whom it's happening. That's just human nature. Well, I wasn't the average human and I didn't try to fool myself. Kevin was a dangerous predator and I could no longer ignore it and let him harm me or someone else.

I listened to increasing pressure from Kevin about trying new sexual activities, and he doubled his efforts to convince me that these were things I needed to try.

There was no time to waste.

I never had a reason before to take notice of just how large the mixing vat was in which we combined the plaster of paris and water for the molds to make the figurines. As I began making my latest survival plan, I spent more and more time looking at the vat, measuring in my mind how I could use the size and shape to my advantage. In the end, I concluded it just might be the tool I needed to get rid of this sick son of a bitch.

The unit was similar to a big chain driven cement mixer and shaped like an upside down Hershey's Kiss. In the manufacturing process, we dumped anywhere from six to twelve hundred pounds of plaster powder in from a huge storage bin next to the work platform at the top, then added water from a hose with a measuring device in the nozzle, to get the formula just right for a perfect mix. An electric motor and attached gear reducer rotated the huge vat with a chain drive and two sprockets sized for the right reduction in revolutions per minute, similar to how you see a cement truck mix the cement and water together. We added more plaster or water while it was mixing, until we achieved the desired consistency to balance curing time, texture and strength. A correct mixture allowed for flexibility which the figurines required to discourage crumbling at the first touch or movement when dry. In other words, they couldn't be too hard. There was a sturdy mixing hoe up on the platform that we used while the mixture was blending, to break up clumps of cement and assure clean and even mixing. It really became an art after working it for a while. Once the mixture churned long enough so all of the plaster and water had mixed thoroughly, with the right consistency and no lumps, we could manually draw the plaster out from the bottom of the vat with a hand-operated sliding shutoff, in the amount needed for each mold. It had to be placed directly beneath the shutoff, usually on a mobile cart made specifically for the mold being used.

Pressure was increasing from Kevin to "experiment" with him, so I decided that the mixing vat would have to serve my purpose, for lack of any better ideas.

I used Kevin's gullibility and eagerness to use me for sex, to slowly turn the tables on him. I did this by pretending he was making progress with me and carefully behaving like I was giving his suggestions some serious thought. I knew that would make him easier to manipulate. He was like he was a kid in a candy store.

I finally told him I might be willing to experiment some, which made him flush with anticipation. He was making himself easier to hate once he let go of all the pretenses. He thought he had me, so for him it was now full speed ahead.

He was positively giddy when I told him that if I was going to experiment with him, it had to be a total secret because if word of it got out, we could both get in trouble. All I had for transportation was a bicycle, so I suggested we should try to meet at the shop, maybe after hours or on Sunday when there was no one else there. He was almost doing a dance, thinking he was going to get a new young boy all to himself. Thinking about how many boys he must have molested over the years strengthened my resolve. This was surely not a new experience for him and whenever I questioned whether I should go through with my plan, thinking of his past victims kept me focused.

Kevin agreed with my idea that it would be better to leave work on Saturday at four, as usual and come back at seven when there was no one around.

I should have been frightened about plotting to kill Kevin, but I wasn't. I guessed anyone else would be scared, but I was as sure of the rightness of this as I had been about Mr. Farmer. Kevin Cooper had to go.

I left work at four, like we planned, but did not go home. I started off in the right direction, but once out of sight of the shop, I scooted down a dirt road and pedaled my bike back toward the rear of the building, stopping on the near end of the field facing the south wall of the shop, to watch. Kevin left about twenty minutes later. Waiting

THE KILLER IN US

was the hard part, but I didn't want to go into the shop early to make the necessary preparations, only to have Kevin come back because he forgot something. After about fifteen minutes, I thought it would be safe to assume that Kevin had gone home. He was probably bathing and dousing himself with cologne in preparation for what he thought was going to be a really big night.

I was becoming very angry because I had just about had my fill of this sick fuck. I scolded myself about my anger because for this to work, I had to seem willing. I knew anger messes with the mind and people don't think clearly when their mind is clouded, so I pushed my anger aside and parked my bike on the opposite side of a stone wall bordering the adjacent field. Making sure my bike couldn't be seen from the street or by anyone from the other direction I made my way to the shop and let myself in.

I didn't turn a light on because there were plenty of safety night lights to illuminate it well enough to see. I climbed the stairway to the platform above the vat, filled it with almost nine hundred pounds of plaster powder, added the required amount of water to make a good mixture and turned the motor on. I had plenty of time yet, so I concentrated on using the mixing hoe to break up any clumps, trying to get the mixture as perfect as I could. It had to be the same mix as anyone operating the machine would strive for when making a normal batch, to avoid arousing suspicion. As seven PM approached, I shut the mixer off and waited quietly for Kevin. I was as calm as a milk-full baby.

At seven o'clock sharp, Kevin's Buick drove up behind the building. He let himself in the side door, looking to see if I was there. He called out my name and I answered from the platform above the vat. He asked what the hell I was doing up there. I answered as playfully as I could that I had decided I was going to play hard to get. He laughed at the fun this was going to be, called me a tease and quickly started up the ladder.

For the first time since I started making my plan for Kevin, I began feeling a little apprehension. Kevin was not a big man, actually shorter than me, but he was an adult and I began to have second thoughts about him being stronger than me. My unexpected fear about that fueled my determination to be sure this worked.

If he could tell that the vat was full from down below, he gave no indication. Perhaps he was so preoccupied with desire that he simply didn't notice, and was only focused on the fun that was waiting for him. I watched him climb the ladder to the landing. As he reached for me, still thinking this was a game, I grabbed his wrist, turned my body away from him and twisted his wrist at the same time, using his own momentum against him. Like the practiced move of a professional wrestler, he flipped completely over me and went head first into the vat of slowly hardening plaster.

He righted himself, more angry than frightened, and asked me what the fuck I had done that for. He yelled at me to help him get out of there, so I picked up the hoe that we used to stir the contents. He saw it in my hands and said it would work good and to hurry and reach it over to him so he could pull himself out before he sank into the mix. He repeatedly shouted that this was not funny.

Instead of reaching out with it so he could grab on, I swung it two-handed like a batter trying for a home run and hit him in the head with the blunt end opposite the blade. It sounded like the flat side of an axe hitting a sandbag and his struggle stopped immediately.

I stood there for what must have been a minute or two and watched as he limply slid into the grey mix like it was quicksand. Then I threw the hoe into the vat too. I carefully looked around to be sure I had left no telltale footprints or any traces of anything that could link me with the events that happened there tonight. Not seeing anything to be fearful of, I climbed down the ladder and without wasting even a moment or a look back, let myself out the same door I had entered. I jumped over the stone wall and rode my bike home in the dark, feeling pretty triumphant that I had faced a hand-to-hand killing like a man. And it had been a success.

Of course, no one went in to work on Sunday, so it was Monday morning and I was in school dealing with Mrs. Starchman, when the full-time workers came in and found the vat filled with hardened plaster of paris. They thought it was odd that Kevin's car was outside the shop and he was nowhere to be found.

It was not long before they became suspicious. Someone went up to the platform and saw the tip of the hoe handle sticking out of the plaster and still no Kevin, so they called the authorities.

Because of their fear that Kevin had somehow fallen into the vat, recovery personnel took off part of the building's roof with the aid of a crane and dismantled the frame supporting the now 1400 pound vat. Then they carefully cut the bowl apart with acetylene torches and chipped away piece by piece at the plaster which was now hardened almost all the way through. I guess the going was tough. When they finally got into it, they found Kevin's body.

They thought he must have come in for some unknown reason to do some manufacturing on his own Saturday night, evidently lost his balance, and fell into the vat while mixing plaster. They further reasoned that he must have hit his head on the side when he fell in, causing him to lose consciousness. The eventual finding was that his death was accidental. This was the final ruling after the investigation, and "That," as they say, was that.

Now, here I was, still only fourteen years old, responsible for, or at least instrumental in the deaths of three people and yet I didn't have one pang of regret, guilt or anguish. I supposed some could call me a murderer, but that would only be people who never walked in my shoes. I only did what weaker people didn't have the stomach for. I didn't go around looking for people to kill, but somehow trouble was always finding me.

It took the plant over five months to reopen after replacing the machinery and rebuilding the framework ruined while recovering Kevin's body, but I never went back to work there. My parents thought it was too dangerous.

Imagine that.

# 9

**M**rs. Starchman continued to make my life miserable at school, but it was a little easier to take, knowing she was next on my list. She still enjoyed singling me out, so I knuckled down, determined to come up with a plan to get rid of this fucking bitch. The more she picked on me, the more I looked forward to evening the score.

Strangely enough, fate sometimes has other plans that you don't see coming and you have to make adjustments.

Nearing the end of the school year, my dad landed a new job in another state. We were going to move to Alabama. I didn't know much about Alabama except I thought they still proudly flew the rebel flag. I guessed I would find out.

To say I was happy to be getting out of that school would be the understatement of the year. It meant, however, that I wouldn't have the time or opportunity to put Mrs. Starchman in that grave I so looked forward to pissing on. This move was extremely fortunate for her because it meant she was going to get a pass. There was only one more month of school and I wouldn't be able to come up with a foolproof plan in that short time, so knowing I would probably never see her again, I reluctantly let her off the hook. She would never know how lucky she was.

Make no mistake, she was staying on my to-do list forever, but only because you never know when life changes again. More than likely, she would have a long life ahead of her to continue being the ugly person she was. I was sure she would find another student to grind on next year.

Other classmates who wanted to get out of the little town of Carpelton envied me, but I reminded them that I was moving to a small town in Alabama, so there probably wouldn't be that much difference. Trying to be upbeat, I reasoned that winters would be warmer and then too, everybody from the south talks funny, so I told myself it might be interesting.

I was happy to be leaving and hoped all the bad I had seen and been subjected to could be left behind so I could get a fresh start. After all, how much worse could people be in Alabama?

Circumstances in my life in Southern Michigan made me do some things I wished I hadn't had to do, but I had no regrets over my actions. I was looking forward to a new beginning surrounded by slow talking, slow walking, easy going Southerners. Perhaps I would meet a pretty Southern Belle too.

More than anything, I hoped for a life among people who didn't need killing. I knew I would do it again if it became necessary, but my new life plan was to take advantage of this opportunity for a new start.

So, right after school let out, we packed up everything we wanted to keep, trashed the rest, said goodbye to Michigan and left for points south.

# 10

We moved on the first of July, to a tiny town in Southern Alabama, near Enterprise and Ozark that made those two speed bumps look big. We moved from a small town in the upper mid-west, barely visible on a map, to one which couldn't even be found on a map.

It was immediately evident, summer was going to be uncomfortable, with oppressive humidity to get used to, but the harder thing was, there was nothing at all to do. They didn't even have a movie theater within driving distance. There were two television stations available and all there was on the radio was some country hillbilly puking about how lonesome he was because his wife left him and his dog died. The funniest thing I found was that all the kids wore straw hats to keep the blistering sun off their heads and nobody wore shoes. I was in Huckleberry Finn Country! If I could be satisfied going fishing barefoot all summer, everything would be good. I wondered how anyone's feet could ever become accustomed to the searing heat of the dirt covering every path and road you used to walk anywhere. And walking was the only mode of transportation. I thought I had died and gone to Hell.

It was so hot that it made no sense to wear a shirt because it would be a wet rag in ten minutes. Also very noticeable was how many people didn't have all of their front teeth. If you walked into the Post Office,

Library or any business and saw an attractive girl there, chances were when she smiled it would be a toothless grin. I assumed they hadn't heard of toothpaste or floss here. There probably wasn't a dentist within 100 miles. If there was, he could have been an extremely rich man.

Thankfully, in less than three weeks, just as I began looking for a railroad depot to hop a freight car out of there, my dad was transferred to another job in yet another place, effective immediately.

I hadn't made any friends in the month I lived in Alabama, so I didn't have any goodbyes to say.

The best news was, my dad's new position was in California! Southern California! We were moving to a little city called Palms. Looking around at the hot dust on the ground and in the air one breathes in Alabama, it sounded like heaven.

In the middle of August, we packed up again and moved to Palms, California, where I once again fostered high expectations of a new start.

We found a home in an apartment complex built on property once designated as housing for soldiers returning home after World War II. It was not the Ritz, but it was fairly new, freshly redecorated, and it wasn't Huck Finn Country. I fell in love with it right away.

Coming from such small town living, to a city where there were actually choices of movie theaters within walking distance, and a downtown area just around the corner, I felt I was finally home. There were movie stars driving right down the streets and beautiful weather all year. This was all I could have hoped for.

Palms was a small city but it was all new to me in that there were no open acres between cities. You just went from one city right into the next, with no way to know except street signs which displayed a different color for each city.

Also, a short bus ride away was Venice Beach, where girls didn't wear many clothes, so for this fifteen-year-old boy, that image occupied most of my thoughts.

School started in September and I found it to be very different from my previous school. They were not nearly as strict, and much more inclined to let a kid be a kid instead of a programmed robot. They treated students like they were young adults with some worth, and it was easy to blend in because it seemed there were hardly any natives. With so many kids coming from somewhere else, as I did, it was easy to mingle, make friends and be comfortable. For the first time since all the negativity from Mrs. Starchman, I began to think I might actually like it.

The first six months went by with not much happening. School was relatively stress-free. I made a few friends including a girlfriend or two and for the first time in a long time, I was enjoying myself. I don't know if it was a culture thing, a natural thing that happens when you get older or what, but the California girls seemed less inhibited about taking off their clothes than the girls back east, so there were rapidly mounting reasons to like this place. Winter was warm, there was very little rain and there was always something to do. I decided I never wanted to move again.

But circumstances can be altered, peace gets disrupted and unforeseen things happen in the blink of an eye.

One night in early March, I walked the few blocks to a small variety store to buy a loaf of bread for my mother. I often went for walks in the evening, usually to have a smoke, but also because there was so much happening and I didn't want to miss any of it. It was never cold, so there was no reason to stay indoors. There were no woods, no ice or snow and no one watching your every move at 8 o'clock at night. For the first time in my life I felt free.

After leaving the store, I walked over to my friend Jimmy's house to visit for a while. We hung around outside and talked about girls, school, girls and more girls. He had never lived in the places where I came from so he was fascinated when I told the stories about Mrs. Starchman and some of the Gestapo tactics I had endured being in her class. We compared girls from other places and came to the conclusion it was no contest. Of course, I never divulged any of my deepest secrets because young I might be, but stupid I wasn't.

By this time it was after nine and it was time for me to leave. I took a short cut through a dark alley so I could get home faster, which I always did. The alley was behind and between businesses, unlit and almost a small block in length, but I wasn't intimidated. I walked through it like a kid without a care in the world.

Almost halfway through the alley, I was accosted by a drunk in smelly, ragged clothes, who wanted me to give him money so he could catch a bus to somewhere.

I don't remember where he wanted to go, possibly Santa Monica, but I knew that any money he managed to panhandle from me wasn't going any further than the liquor store on the front side of the block. He probably wanted to buy more booze to ensure a few more hours in the drunken fog he was swirling in. When I told him to get lost, he became violent, roughly grabbing my arm and twisting me around.

I dropped the bag of bread and swung my right fist, all in one motion, hitting him in the face. He fell backwards, cracking his head against the brick building behind him on his way down. When he hit the ground, his head slammed on the concrete and bounced just once, making a sound similar to someone dropping a water balloon from a high place. He didn't move.

I retrieved the bag of bread and got the hell gone from there.

When I arrived home, I gave my mother her bread and never breathed a word of what happened with the drunk in the alley.

I didn't know if he was seriously injured, temporarily knocked out when he fell or just passed out from too much booze. I didn't think I had hit him all that hard, but he was so drunk that if I had missed him, the wind from the punch probably would have knocked him over. I put it out of my head.

When I saw Jimmy in school the next day, he said I should have stuck around to see the excitement after I left. I asked him what he was talking about. He said they found a dead guy in the alley across from his house last night.

My heart fell to the ground. Could this be? No doubt it must have been the drunk who accosted me. Perhaps something happened when he hit his head on the brick or the pavement. I didn't think I had hit him hard enough to kill him, but he was dead and if there were any witnesses who could identify me, I would still be held accountable for it.

And here I was, thinking I was turning over a new leaf and starting a better life. Now it felt like the old one was following me. Perhaps ridding the world of bad people was going to be my purpose in life, but I didn't even know this man. I knew nothing about him other than he was falling-down drunk in a dark alley. I didn't know whether he was a bad guy or a really good person who simply drank too much, but there he was, dead at my hand. It didn't make me feel very good.

The only way I could wrap my head around this was with the knowledge that he accosted me and not the other way around. He was the one who decided to get rough in that alley. I was minding my own business, but even though I knew it was clearly a case of self-defense, I still had another notch on my gun.

I wondered if this thing of killing people was going to be a regular activity for me. If my purpose in life was going to be to kill bad people, so be it. It wasn't like I was being offered a choice.

Still, I had no one to talk with about this. After much soul searching, I decided this was no worse than the others I had killed, so I put the unwarranted guilt in its proper place. It was dark, there were no witnesses and at that time the government didn't have surveillance cameras watching your every move, so I thought I was pretty safe. There was no way anyone could connect me with his death.

I never found out what the authorities concluded about the dead man in the alley. I assumed they must have decided he was just a drunk who had passed out, struck his head on either the bricks or the pavement when he fell, and died from head trauma. There was no evidence to prove otherwise and I wasn't going to volunteer anything. I just kept my mouth shut, put another terrible experience behind me and moved on. I hoped it would end here.

# 11

As luck would have it, in just eight short months, my dad got yet another job transfer. This transfer was to Tucson, Arizona and it meant we were moving to another small town. This one was named Top Rock. It was another jerkwater town somewhere between Tucson and the Sierrita Mountains. Top Rock, Arizona didn't rate a dot on the Rand McNally either. The news came as a severe blow. I thought I was going to be set for life in what I thought was paradise and instead I had to say goodbye to peekaboo bikinis and hello to dust and cactus flower spines.

My dad left right away, but we stayed in California until the end of the school year. Then it was off to Arizona, or as I learned to call it, Arid Zona. It was very hot and dirty everywhere. Locals were staunchly defending it, saying it was a dry heat, but I thought that was akin to saying your house burned down, but it was a dry fire. I spent the summer loafing and began my junior year in September with a chip on my shoulder the size of Rhode Island. I didn't like it there, didn't want to be there and didn't care who knew it. This landed me in trouble on my first day of school.

I was enrolled in a World History class with a Native Arizonian teacher who couldn't lay claim to having been anywhere except the nowhere town this was, but thought he was a man of the world. When I told him where I transferred in from, he made it clear to me and the class that California, in his opinion, was truly the "Land of Fruits and Nuts." I answered with a remark that at least it meant living in a civilized place where you weren't tracking horse shit into the tepee every day. He took offense to that, so there I was, being sent to the principal's office on my very first day of school. Evidently they didn't have guidance counselors in Arizona. That was too bad, because I was pretty well experienced in how to deal with guidance counselors.

I received a lecture about this town being a wholesome place and that the loose morals I may have grooved on in California were not going to be tolerated in my new school.

I took my lecture like a man and went back to class. My teacher seemed satisfied that I had been set straight, but that wasn't exactly the case with all of my peers.

On the third day in my new school, I was approached in the bathroom by two other boys about my attitude. They were Native American Indians, from one local tribe or other who had taken offense to my reference about bringing horse shit into the tepee, and they evidently thought I needed a lesson in respect. They proceeded to punch and kick me and didn't stop until I was leaking blood on the floor, holding tightly to two cracked ribs. I later found out I also had a concussion and a few loosened teeth.

When they were convinced that they had beaten the disrespect out of me, they washed my blood off their hands and walked away. Someone called my parents and an ambulance, not necessarily in that order, and they took me to the emergency room in an adobe style building that they called a hospital. There wasn't anything they could do for the rib pain or the loose teeth, but I spent three days in the hospital, because of lingering symptoms from the concussion. It had left me dizzy and nauseous, but not enough to keep me from plotting my revenge. I thought I was putting all of that behind me, and I really wanted to, but clearly these yahoos were just two more bullies who got their jollies from punching and kicking people caught off guard and outnumbered. I was going to have a little surprise for them. Little did they know I had ways of dealing with their kind. Bullying was a behavior I simply wouldn't tolerate. Beating me up just opened a can of worms for them in a place called pain that they didn't know existed. They would find out.

I was asked by the authorities to identify my assailants, but I of course refused, saying I thought things would just get worse for me if I told on them. The law enforcement people were probably from the same tribe, so they didn't seem overly concerned. They were going to protect their own and were just as happy I wouldn't talk. This way, they weren't forced to pursue it. Of course, my dad was still very much disconnected from the family and likewise, my mom, as usual, thought I should have run away screaming for help. They offered no words of encouragement over my beating, but I expected nothing different.

I could say the names of the boys who beat me up, but I preferred to think of them as Beaver Shit and Buffalo Dung. They were big old desert dwelling assholes whose only enjoyment in life was clunking around in dirty cowboy boots and beating up city folks.

Living there was boring because there was nothing to do but watch the grass grow, if you could find any grass, so I had a lot of time to think things through and plan for their comeuppance.

Beaver Shit was the bigger and most vicious of the two, but Buffalo Dung had done his share too, so he wasn't getting a pass. And I could be patient. I knew that if something was to happen to either of them right away, I would be a prime suspect. This wasn't my first experience in this kind of thing. I suspected the local law enforcement people knew exactly who had beaten me up, but they were all related and here I was, a wise-ass white kid who had the nerve to voice a not-so-glowing opinion of their home town. They probably agreed with Beaver Shit and Buffalo Dung that the insult just couldn't be overlooked.

# 12

Time marched on, here I was in eleventh grade and my troubles had finally settled down some. I grew quickly that year to a height of a little over six feet and I filled out nicely, with mostly muscle. I also decided it was time to hone my ability to defend myself, should I ever be in another unfair situation where I might need some fighting skills. Being outnumbered makes for a difficult defense, but it can be done.

Taking boxing lessons or judo or other classes like that would cast suspicion and maybe even invite trouble and until I was ready, I wanted to keep a low profile. I purposely stayed away from Buffalo Dung and Beaver Shit.

I began training myself and learning as much as I could about fighting. Watching professional boxing gave me many pointers about how to block punches and how to take advantage of your opponent's weaknesses. In my case, I had excellent reflexes and I felt I had a natural ability in the defensive department. I began focusing on punching power and strengthening my legs. I enjoyed watching a young man from Kentucky named Clay fight. He had the moves and the strength that I wanted to develop. I marveled at his timing and conditioning and while I couldn't guess if I would ever need all this training, I was sure of one thing: I was never going to take a beating like that again. You could say I had found incentive.

I bought a speed bag at a yard sale, found a heavy bag at the Salvation Army and brought them home, deciding it was time to learn to fight. Between pounding on the heavy bag in our basement and whacking the speed bag in our garage, my knuckles were taking quite a beating, so I got a pair of padded gloves from a sporting goods store which weren't too expensive. At least they kept the skin on my knuckles.

It wasn't long before I realized that while I had a natural ability for speed and agility, I was never going to be a pure power puncher. With determination I continued to hit those bags with everything I had, in every spare minute I could find, as long as my fists and wrists would stand it.

I became quite fascinated with professional boxing and professional wrestling. I knew wrestling was faked, but it wasn't long before it planted the idea that for what I needed to do, fighting dirty was not at all out of the question. If it was going to come down to a physical confrontation, the objective would simply be to win. How that was accomplished was not important. There is no fair way to fight. There is just a winner and a loser. And I was not going to be the loser.

Looking back on what I did to Kevin in the plaster vat, you could hardly have called that a fair fight. It was simply a matter of survival. The method I chose was a means to an end. Nothing more, nothing less. If I had failed, the unanswered question was, what would Kevin have done to me? Suppose I had been the one to go into the vat? It was self-evident that once you start something like this, you have to finish it in any way you can. Fairness isn't a consideration.

In the meantime, because I stayed under the radar, people didn't seem to notice that I was putting on pounds and getting pretty muscular. It's surprising how if you stay out of the spotlight, people don't even see you.

I always had a girlfriend, but at the same time I didn't really want one. There were a couple of girls I dated, mostly to go with to movies, or if I was lucky, to spend play time with when their parents weren't home. Occasionally I met with one girl in particular on the west side, where there was privacy in the more sparsely settled parts of the town. We had occasional sexual dalliances, and I was not looking for anything more than what these meetings were. The girls eventually caught on that I was a loner, so except for a couple of them who were always ready for sex, interest waned. Most of the girls I dated were hunting for a steady boyfriend, while I was simply looking to get laid. I knew that eventually there could and would be trouble coming to me, perhaps trouble which would make me light out because I was in a mess with the law.

I didn't want to be distracted from my goals nor did I want some girl all brokenhearted when one day I was just gone. So I kept my relationships at arm's length.

# 13

Now I was a senior and I had yet to settle the scores with Beaver Shit and Buffalo Dung. I knew the time might be getting right because of some friction they were having between them. It seems Buffalo Dung had a girlfriend and Beaver Shit, being the sleaze bag that he was, couldn't stay away from her and wouldn't leave her alone. Then I heard that the girl dumped Buffalo Dung for Beaver Shit and Buffalo Dung wasn't very happy about it. Evidently the girlfriend and Beaver Shit were screwing each other long before she broke up with Buffalo Dung, adding to the friction between them. I thought I saw the crack I needed to settle an old score. I wondered if I might be able to pit them against each other and at the same time, avoid putting myself in the spotlight.

I waited for what seemed like an eternity to see what would happen between them and finally came to the conclusion that while these two might be bullies, they were also cowards. It was easy for them to be brave when beating up on me and who knows how many others in a two-against-one fight. I had been, and probably still was considered an easy mark, as I did my best to just blend in. I wore the cowboy boots now, just like all the other kids, but kept a low profile because I knew what I was planning, and I wanted to be the last person anyone would suspect. Who was it said, ignore the loudmouth, but beware the quiet one? Whoever he was, he must have been talking about me.

Unfortunately the time was not quite right yet, so I waited patiently. I knew I would recognize when the time was right, but a few more things had to happen first. I continued to wait.

While I was biding my time, life went on. I needed the things that all teenagers need which cost money, so I got a part-time job at a photo shop. It didn't pay much, but all I needed was enough for smokes and a car. There was no way get laid very often without a car, so I saved my money for a few weeks, then bought an old, very used Plymouth, for sixty-five dollars. It was ugly and showed more rust than paint, but it would take me from point A and get me to point B without too much trouble. As long as it had four wheels and a back seat, I was happy.

A lot had happened since our move to Arizona. Our country's president was assassinated, followed by a massive cover-up about how it happened and why. I never doubted that there were at least two shooters who killed President Kennedy. Our government's dogged insistence that it wasn't a conspiracy didn't quell my fears at all. It just made me begin to suspect my own government, because despite all of the wide speculation realistic theories and photos suggesting otherwise, they were never going to tell us the truth. I applauded Jack Ruby for killing Lee Harvey Oswald because I was getting tired of bad people fucking around with good people and trying to ruin our country. But I wanted desperately to learn who helped Oswald do this awful thing. I was never satisfied with the government's lame answers and stubborn insistence that Oswald acted alone. I was just a kid, but although I might have been born at night, it wasn't last night. Videos everyone saw told a different story from the one they wanted us to believe. Even at the young age of seventeen, I looked forward to growing up and moving to Dallas, finding out who the other son of a bitch was who assassinated President Kennedy, and killing him too. But I would be smarter than Jack Ruby. I did not need notoriety or publicity. I just planned on killing him and walking away with no one ever finding out who did it. Knowing I killed the bastard who murdered our President would be satisfaction enough for me.

We had a new President who struck me right off as a bit of a bumbler, although I always thought he meant well. Things to test his mettle started to heat up in a little country half way around the world called Vietnam which most of us had never heard of. My father kept saying it was going to be our next war.

For lack of anything else to do, I started watching Beaver Shit whenever I could, to see if he had developed any pattern that might give me an opening. I had been waiting a long time to settle the score and it felt like the time was getting close. I came to grips with the fact that I was lucky a couple of times and if this time the confrontation had to be hand-to-hand, I thought I had a few huge advantages.

First, any action by me would come as a surprise. I had kept a low profile since these two assholes ganged up on me, so I was sure they wrote me off as some pussy they had intimidated. They thought I was just a harmless sissy who they scared away. Second, was all of the muscle mass I had gained from working out. I was a little over six feet tall, weighed about two-hundred pounds and none of it was fat. I worked hard and it paid off, so there was no fear factor about getting physical with these goons. I was confident I could beat either of them in an even fight. The third advantage I had now was that I was going to fight dirty. As dirty as I needed to fight. I was prepared to do whatever it took, and I planned to make it quick.

With the territorial pride that precipitated the awful beating those two gave me over my insults about their crappy little town, you would think they lived on big cattle ranches or something similar. In reality, Beaver Shit did live in a rural area, because that's about all there was, but they did not have cattle. They had chickens. Perhaps that's why he had a chip on his shoulder. He must have thought that by being a tough guy, no one would have the balls to call him a chicken farmer. When I found this out, I thought it was quite funny. He acted like his after-school job might be as a wrangler or something, when in reality all he did was take chickenfeed to the henhouse twice a day.

Beaver Shit lived about a mile-and-a-half from me and even though I had a driver's license and a car, I drove only part of the way to his house, then hiked the last half mile to the chicken farm to watch him. Driving my car there would be too conspicuous and too easy for someone to remember. There wasn't much cover as you got closer to his house, so it just made more sense to park in a supermarket lot where no one would pay any attention, and go the rest of the way on foot.

The Tucson/Yuma area and most all of the rest of Southern Arizona doesn't have a lot of vegetation to hide behind. It's mostly cactus, rocks, sand and dust, but I needed to watch him. As often as I could, I hoofed it over to his house, keeping myself off the roads and away from anyone's house or dog and then I sat in a patch of weeds and cactus and watched his house. They had two chicken houses and every night, when it was almost dark, Beaver Shit would go out, round up the chickens in the pen and herd them into the coops. Then he would lock them in for the night after making sure they had food and water, and then go back to his house.

I planned and planned, but could not come up with a sure-fire way to do what I wanted to do and still have an alibi that would be solid if anyone started looking at me. I also had to make a plan B in case the original plan failed. You can never count on your opponent to follow the script in your head, so you better know what you are going to do when they don't.

Then, the best thing that could have happened did. Buffalo Dung finally reached his boiling point over being dumped for Beaver Shit, laid in waiting after school and he and Beaver Shit finally had it out. I did not see it, but word spread around that Beaver Shit laid a terrible beating on Buffalo Dung. From what I heard, people had to break it up because Beaver Shit would not stop after he got the upper hand. Perhaps Buffalo Dung thought that because he was the one who was wronged, he would naturally be the victor. It turned out he learned a lesson the hard way that being in the right doesn't mean squat. Buffalo Dung got beaten up pretty badly.

It was also an exercise in futility, because it didn't get him his girlfriend back. She was evidently a piece of work in her own right and despised him afterward for picking a fight with her new boyfriend. Go figure.

My opening was finally here. Buffalo Dung had motive.

One night, about three weeks after the big fight, while it was still wintery and as cold as it gets there, with darkness coming early, following Plan A, I went directly after school to take up my hiding place near the chicken yard where I couldn't be seen. I waited for the Beaver Shit to come out to tend to his chickens. The only Plan B I had was an old ax handle which I brought in case Plan A fizzled.

When it was almost dark and I knew he would be coming out soon, I left my hiding place and ran around to the north side of the chicken coop the furthest away from his house and waited there. In the place I chose to confront him, no one would be able to see us, from either the road or his house. With no one able to see us in this location, I was confident that nobody but Beaver Shit and I would ever know what went down.

I knew I was taking a mighty big chance, but I had planned this all out for so long, taking into consideration every imaginable scenario and what my action for his reaction would be. I finally got it down to what I thought would seem like it was scripted. I was very confident of my physical abilities and at this point, thought I could take Beaver Shit in a stand up fight. But I wasn't going to make it a stand up fight.

I also thought that if it went all wrong and I was discovered, not having brought a gun or a knife, who wouldn't believe I had just gone there to fight him with my fists. No one would notice anything unusual about the presence of an old ax handle on a farm.

Ten minutes or so later, Beaver Shit came out to the closest chicken coop, rounded up his birds and locked the door after the chickens scampered up their little stepped ramp. He walked down to where I was hiding in the shadow. I had carefully placed the ax handle deep in the shadow, within easy reach, but not so easy to see.

When he got to the corner of the coop, he saw me standing there and came up short. Startled, he said, "What the fuck are you doing here?

I mumbled "I'm sorry," quietly, so he could not hear exactly what I had said.

He looked at me incredulously and said, "What, didn't you get enough last time?" He was obviously still feeling his oats from his big win against his former friend and thought he might enjoy beating me up again. He spread his feet and braced himself to land a blow.

I repeated, "I'm sorry," again, low enough that he could not quite hear.

He instinctively leaned toward me to try to catch what I was saying. When he did, I swung my right foot with the pointed cowboy boot into his groin like I was kicking the winning field goal in the Championship Game. It was a perfect kick. He grabbed his newly crushed balls, bent over like his top half and lower half were hinged and turned white as a sheet. As he bent over, he cast a pained look at me and I kicked him again, this time in the face, catching him right at the point of his jaw with the wooden heel of my boot. He went down like a cheap marionette whose strings were suddenly cut. It turned out I didn't even need to use the ax handle.

It was a very satisfying beat down, taking this piece of shit on without a weapon and hardly a whimper. I quickly bent over him to see if he was just unconscious or dead. He was breathing and I thought with the force of the kick to his jaw, he was going to be out for a while. He had rolled on his side when he fell, so I moved behind him, squatted down and put my knee into the back of his neck. Then I reached around with my left hand and covered his mouth, while pinching his nose shut with two fingers on my right hand. There was very little struggle to speak of and in about a minute, he went completely limp, so I knew he was dead. I held on for another minute to be sure, then checked for a pulse and found none. I didn't take time to admire my work. I wanted to just run, but I knew I had to make sure no one had seen me and that I wasn't leaving any sign which could point to me. Of course, if someone had seen me, I didn't know that there was much I could have done about it.

Looking around at the hard packed dirt by the entrance to the chicken yard and where our short confrontation took place, I knew there would be no identifiable footprints and I had never touched anything that would have left a fingerprint. After standing stock still for a minute, and hearing no evidence of activity anywhere, I grabbed up the ax handle and lit a shuck for home.

And once again, I slept like a baby.

As I had hoped, Buffalo Dung quickly became the prime suspect in Beaver Shit's death because of the awful beating he had received over the slutty girlfriend. Almost everyone in Arizona wore cowboy boots that had similarly shaped soles and heels, so the scuffed footprints left at the scene offered no workable evidence. They never found tire tracks or anything to indicate there was more than one person involved, and there were no witnesses.

I was never suspected, or if I was, I never knew about it. Buffalo Dung wound up not having any charges pressed against him because other than having motive, there was no proof that he had done it. He had a weak alibi that held up, so even though the investigation still pointed to him, there was really no solid proof.

As I had in my previous adventures, after the deed was done and another predator had been removed, I distanced myself from anything that might throw suspicion my way. To my knowledge, they never brought charges against anyone, so his murder was never solved.

Score another one for the good guys.

# 14

Prom night came and went and graduation followed. I had a wonderful date for the prom, but unlike what many kids expect on that occasion, I didn't get drunk or laid. My date was a beautiful girl named Linda, and I liked her more than she will ever know, but a relationship like that was out of the question for me. I didn't want to have an emotional connection only for it turn to shit if I had to skip town one step ahead of the authorities. With my past, who knew if or when that would happen.

I wanted to leave this one-horse town one way or another and the sooner the better. It wasn't in my plan to live with my parents and make a Spartan living at the photo shop.

So, despite wanting to get laid on Prom night, we just had a wonderful, fun evening with no expectations.

When graduation came, unlike other kids who were getting jobs or going on to college, I was not. Instead, I joined the Army.

The recruiter promised golden opportunities for me, while stressing the privilege of serving my Country at the same time. With the offer of three squares a day, a bed to sleep on and a starting salary of about $175.00 a month with no living expenses, it sounded like a good deal, so I signed the papers.

My dad, in a rare moment of praise, said he would be proud to have a soldier in the family. My mom wept. The few friends I had thought I was crazy to join the Army, but in reality that was because they were all afraid to enlist. They were trying to ignore the Military Draft that affected every male between the ages of 18 and 35. Our country required every able bodied young man to serve six years of military service, so sooner or later, they were going to have to enlist or be drafted.

The recruiter told me that enlisting instead of being drafted would allow me to make my own choice of what career I wanted to pursue as a soldier. I wanted to be in the Infantry because if there was fighting, that is where I was best suited. I had proven my ability and my nerve to myself with the events in my past.

More than once I had experienced fear and the anticipation of fear and I passed any personal tests I might have had. The Army wanted people who weren't afraid to kill, and I could kill. They needed people like me. I was good at it.

I enlisted as an E-1 pay grade Private and was sent to Ft. Benning, Georgia for 10 weeks of Basic Training. I looked forward to joining the Army as just a yokel off the street one day, and ten short weeks later, leaving Basic Training as a well-trained soldier.

They flew me from Tucson to Phoenix to Chicago to Atlanta and bused about twenty-five of us, mostly draftees, from the airport to the Army Fort. By the time I arrived there, the heat of that July afternoon had become stifling. We gingerly got off the bus only to be greeted by the biggest, ugliest, meanest black men I had ever seen. They screamed every word that came from their mouths and called us for every motherfucker, jerkoff, cocksucker that ever lived. They were relentless in their verbal attack and seemed to have no idea how hot it was, how confused we were, or how terribly uncomfortable they were making us. Looking back on it later, I think they knew exactly how hot it was, how confused we were and how terribly uncomfortable they were making us.

I had every expectation that it would be tough, but the recruiter never said anything about abuse. It wasn't long before I began to experience buyer's remorse, thinking I might have made a terrible mistake by enlisting.

They made us stand at attention in a sweltering parking lot on hot asphalt for a good hour that first day before they wound down even a little on the screaming. I didn't think they were slowing down out of affection for us, but rather because their voices were stretched to the limit. The incessant swearing didn't stop. It just wasn't quite as loud. Then they started separating the masses, categorizing us by whether we were enlistees or draftees. They now had two groups of recruits and although they were still nasty, they softened just the smallest bit on the enlistees. Like they thought enlistees were respectful enough to volunteer to serve in their beloved Army. They didn't back off an inch with the lowly draftees who they felt they had to go fetch. Oh, we were still all vermin, but I guess the draftees were just considered a lower class of cocksucker.

It was 2 A.M. before we were assigned to barracks. We were given one set of fatigues and underwear and told to wear them in the morning. The problem was, it was already the next morning and I was so tired and confused I could barely stand up. I didn't get into a bunk until three but it didn't matter much because their screaming and swearing woke us at five. Then they had the balls to say we should be thankful that they let us sleep in.

For the first couple of days we were processed in and had physicals again, getting shots for who knows what, having eyes and hearing tested again, blood typed again and more blood drawn. I wondered what they did with all that blood. I overheard one draftee saying the Drill Sergeants probably put it on their cornflakes. Of course, what kind of a first day would it be without having your prostate checked one more time.

I wondered if they had a contest to see which medic had the fattest fingers for that particular exam. I was very tired, but even when we were finished with the poking and prodding and all that went with it, if it was still daylight, we were not allowed to lie down on our bunks.

After about four days of bullshit and browbeating, we were finally placed in a Basic Training Company. In stifling heat, they crammed us into what can only be described as cattle cars, and drove us around in circles to be sure we were completely disoriented. When we arrived at our new Company Area, we disembarked and the screaming and personal attacks began anew. We were assigned to platoons and marched off to new barracks which would be our home for the next eight or nine weeks.

We received our first lecture within an hour of our arrival about how we had better forget about our Mommies, Daddies and Blowjob Annie back home. Our asses now belonged to these awful men and we had better get that through our heads right now.

Our Drill Sergeant, a well sculpted black man told us that beginning tomorrow morning, we would arise at three o'clock, get our bunks made, clean the barracks and wash and buff the floors every morning, then get ourselves squared away before falling out at five. We would double-time four miles before breakfast for the first three days and after that, we would increase to six miles before chow.

Naturally, I thought he was joking. He was not.

He laid out rules such as, no food allowed in the barracks and informed us that the Army is only required to give us eight hours for which to sleep every night. Of course, in that eight hours' time, you also had to do your laundry, shine your boots, polish your brass, write home, and anything else which needed doing. There were to be no phone calls home, even if we could find a pay phone to use.

Naturally, I thought he was joking. He was not.

When they fed us, we had to eat everything we were served and no more. The only thing they allowed seconds on was milk. I guess we needed the calcium.

At night, we were required to take turns in one hour shifts to be on "fire watch." I supposed that was in case some yahoo fell asleep smoking in his bunk. Of course, you weren't allowed to smoke sitting on your bunk even during the day, but there is always some idiot who tests the rules. They said they didn't give a shit if we all died in a fire, but the wood to build new barracks was expensive.

The barracks where we were housed was a two- story wooden structure from World War II that gave the illusion that there were two roofs. They were old, but they were solid. There were monkey bar setups outside, for those of us who needed to practice more than others and the latrine consisted of a room with a pissing trough on one wall, and six sinks on the opposite wall. The third wall was lined with toilets. There were no stalls or doors affording any privacy, just toilets. The fourth wall was the shower area, which was also just a big room with a dozen shower heads on the wall and three floor drains.

There was no shortage of disciplinary measures taken when someone was stupid enough to be a wise ass. Push-ups by the dozens was the favorite because it was so easy for a D.I. to say, "Drop and give me fifty, motherfucker." I wondered if they were taught this at Drill Instructor School or it was something they thought up on their own, because it seemed to be the universal punishment. If you so much as sneezed, you were on your face doing fifty.

Another punishment was to make a wayward recruit run in circles around the perimeter of the Company Area, arms flapping, yelling, "I'm a Gooney Bird!!" After twenty to fifty laps of this, depending on the infraction, the recruit saw things in a new light.

If someone was dumb enough to put a cigarette out by stepping on it and leaving the butt there, they were in for a big surprise. The punishment for that infraction was to dig a six-by-six-by-six foot hole, bury the butt and fill in the hole. Then you had to pray over the cigarette's "grave." You were only allowed to use your Army issue entrenching tool, which in reality was just a small, foldable shovel with a short handle. That usually took an entire day, even in the sandy soil at the training center. Anyone who thinks that would be easy should try it.

After the first day I correctly guessed they were simply trying to break us. In many cases they did. When we figured that out, things began to flow a little smoother. I simply blocked out all of the screaming and swearing and didn't let these huge black men intimidate me. There were many recruits who were terrified and the Drill Sergeants, having a knack for spotting the gutless ones, quickly zeroed in on the patsies. The weak and frightened took the brunt of the harassment.

For the most part, I would like to have thought the Drill Sergeants were just doing a job, but there were a few who enjoyed it too much. I wondered if you had to be a sadist to qualify for the job. There was one particular sick son of a bitch, who stood out. Sergeant Kellen was a fat white Staff Sergeant who looked like Baby Huey. The louder he screamed, the higher pitched his voice became until he sounded like a raving lunatic. I don't think that analogy was far off.

I watched him brutally beat up recruits many times in the first week of training. Being on the receiving end of a beat down from him when he was off his rocker was not unusual for the pussies in the troop because they were the ones who were picked on the most. The pleasure he received from hurting young, unsuspecting recruits who didn't know any better wasn't something you can train someone for. His brutality and the delight he derived from it far exceeded his authority. He reminded me of a grown-up Donny Blackmon with the authority to destroy people.

Rumor had it that he was crazy with fear because after this cycle, he was being shipped out to Southeast Asia, so he didn't care if he was court martialed for brutality. That just told me that he was a coward as well as a bully. But of course, my experiences proved that most bullies are born cowards anyway.

He never physically hurt me, but as time went on and I saw the things he got away with, I started having serious thoughts about how I could make an accident happen when we finally got to weapons training. A stray bullet there could make the world a better place.

As it turned out, when we were finally introduced to an actual firearm, it was an M14 rifle that fired standard NATO 7.62mm full metal jacketed ammunition. The metal jacketed bullet looked like it could penetrate a steel bunker, much less kill a man. The M14 rifle had a kick that made it lethal at both ends. I did not like it.

# 15

Ten weeks spent in Basic Training instilled a mental toughness in us that most of us didn't know we possessed. I knew I wasn't a pushover, but if I wasn't a killing machine before, I was now.

Every day consisted of push-ups, sit-ups, forced marches, drilling, shooting, bayonet practice and more. It sounds a little over the top, but it is meant to mold you into an efficient killer. Little did they know they were dealing with someone who was already capable of killing. Then they showed me how to do it better.

Basic was winding down and there were still guys crying for their mommies every night, but there was a general hardness in the rest of us. My experiences and the things I saw made me decide that if I got the chance to get rid of Sgt. Kellen before this was over, I would. Unfortunately, I never saw the opening, but I still felt he shouldn't have been allowed to breathe the same air as good people. I saw nothing wrong with getting rid of this despicable man. He used his rank to hurt and maim weaker men and the Army seemingly approved, because I never saw him reprimanded There was a long line of recruits sent to the hospital after being smacked in the jaw with a rifle butt, kicked, punched and thrown off obstacle courses, and he continued to deliberately inflict injury on the weaker of the troops, even though we were nearing the end of our training. Sergeant Kellen was a bully in need of killing.

Finally, Basic Training was over and it was on to Advanced Infantry Training. I stayed at Ft. Benning for that as well, but did not see many guys from Basic, so it was like starting over. I was much saltier now and not taking shit from anyone, but everyone there was of the same mind, so we understood each other.

AIT was mostly a continuation of Basic only instead of being treated like a raw recruit you were given the respect worthy of a soldier. Long marches, hours on the firing range, hand-to-hand combat exercises and in-depth bayonet training beyond what we had learned in Basic, became the order of the day. When asked what the purpose was of the bayonet, we screamed, "To Kill! Kill! Kill!"

As you can imagine, this suited me just fine. You could say I already had some experience in that line of work and by this time I was convinced that justifiable homicide was going to be my specialty in life.

Ten weeks of Advanced Infantry Training and I was like a well-oiled killing machine. I felt like I was faster than a locomotive and could leap tall buildings at a single bound. There was nothing I couldn't do and my mental toughness was only exceeded by my physical abilities. Between Basic and AIT I had put on 20 more pounds and all of it was muscle. I was no longer the tall skinny kid who kept to himself, but a hungry killer of men, looking for a place to put my skills to good use.

There was a place to do just that. It was a little country in Southeast Asia, called Vietnam. And it was heating up there despite little knowledge of it.

A two week furlough came first, and I went home to say goodbye to my family before heading out to war. A visit home was like going back in time to a place I didn't belong. I was not the same person who left there five months ago. My parents still lived in Arizona and there was still nothing to do when I got there. I had never cultivated any friendships, didn't have a girlfriend to go see and it was still hot and dusty. So there was nothing to do but wait to ship out.

When in Basic and AIT, I always laughed when the Chaplain would tell us not to get mixed up with "Susie the Floozie," meaning one of the girls who could be found right off base, wanting to latch on to a government dependent support check. Instead, we were encouraged to save ourselves and marry the girl back home. Wasn't she "Blowjob Annie," the one the drill instructors told us to forget on that first day of Basic? I thought perhaps the Chaplain didn't know about her.

I didn't have a girl back home and I never got involved with the spousal support hunters lurking off base, so that conflicting advice always gave me a chuckle.

I had a healthy interest in girls, but knowing the line of work I had been in since I could remember I still had no desire for a long-term relationship. I dated, mostly to take care of physical needs. But my true motivation was to go on to what I considered to be my purpose in life. There were a lot of people who needed killing and from what I was taught in AIT, there were more than I could imagine. They were wearing black pajamas and killing Americans in Vietnam. I thought I could help my country, so I couldn't wait to get started.

When my furlough was finally over, I couldn't get out of Arizona fast enough. I left, vowing to never go back there again, at least not to the hot, dusty southern part of the state. One of the most important things I learned from living there was that when it's hot, you need shade and to have shade, you need trees. Southern Arizona had very few trees.

# 16

A short flight to San Francisco, a very long flight to Okinawa, and one more flight landed me in Da Nang, South Vietnam where the air smelled like a combination of smoke and shit. The war-scarred landscape looked like Mars with palm trees and the people were all midgets. I was getting my wish.

I was assigned to the 101st Tactical Infantry Division, probably named after a similar division from WWII. I was promoted to Private First Class a day before we shipped out to a place called Dak To. I wondered who made up these names in the Vietnamese language. The words all looked like they were concocted by people who couldn't spell.

As I wandered through the mass of soldiers stationed there, I surprisingly ran into a couple of guys I had served with in basic training at Ft. Benning. It made me feel almost at home to talk with someone I could relate to. As bad as that time was, we had the experience in common. We hadn't been buddies in Basic, but it was good to see a familiar face or two in this new home halfway around the world. Much to my surprise, they said we were in the same outfit as that fucking lunatic, Sgt. Kellen from Basic Training. Surely, this couldn't be coincidence. What were the crazy odds that of all the places in the Army to be stationed, I would wind up in his outfit. It was like there was another power controlling my life, showing me that I really did have a calling.

I had plenty of pent-up hatred for Kellen and I still thought he needed killing, but I had to get a feel for the danger here first. I might need this asshole to cover my back, and he couldn't cover my back if he was dead. I also knew better than to let hatred go unchecked. To successfully avenge wrongdoing, you had to have your thoughts together and your emotions under control. Going off half-cocked usually makes you just another criminal who gets caught because he was stupid. I didn't think I was a criminal, because I only killed people when it was necessary. Law enforcement might think otherwise, but I always knew I was right. I wasn't a crazy, who heard voices in the night or a nut case seeking release from an overbearing mother, I was sane, kind and compassionate. I simply killed bad people when the need arose.

Shortly after arriving at Dak To, we knew there was a battle shaping up because we heard talk of being ordered to take three hills. As asinine as it sounds, instead of names, the Army assigned numbers to targets and they numbered three hills from which we were supposed to drive the enemy. Hills 823, 724 and 882 were evidently of some importance and we were ordered to shoot as many of these little pajama wearing bastards called Charlie as we could or at least make them run off into the jungle, so we could claim these hills as our own. It sounded stupid then and still did, after over 300 American soldiers died in the times we took these hills, gave them back and took them again. I quickly found out there wasn't much in that war that made any sense.

They flew us to a Landing Zone near hill 823 in a helicopter UH-1, affectionately called a Huey. Those who weren't sick with fear got sick from the turbulence. It was not the way I had envisioned going into combat but it was what it was. And John Wayne wasn't there.

We landed on what at first appeared to be a field, but had actually been woods cleared ahead of our arrival for a landing zone to land the helicopters carrying infantrymen. We touched down safely and set up a headquarters, which amounted to the Lieutenant in charge and communications. Nobody slept that night for fear of being attacked in the dark when we weren't prepared. Everyone was scared, including me. We didn't want to get our feet wet in the dark.

We were attacked, but it was mid-morning when the attack came. It was a half-hearted effort where they shot at us and we shot back at them and I don't think anyone was killed or wounded on either side. Suffering no casualties in our first brush with the enemy did wonders for our confidence. With our heads held high and chests now puffed out, we thought we were going to go out there, kick ass and take names.

What we didn't know yet was that Charlie was just feeling out our strength and readiness. I think they found out we were ready.

Crazy Sgt. Kellen was a platoon leader for the third platoon. I had seen him and even spoken with him the day after I arrived, but he didn't appear to remember me. If he did remember me, he didn't let on. He still carried the crazed look on his face which I could see was fear. Looking back on it, I think it was stark raving terror on the face of a crazy man that anyone should have been able to see. He was as nuts as a man could be and still function. I never understood how he could have been placed in charge of a platoon of twenty-six troops on a combat mission. Perhaps he had proven himself in combat in the two months he was there before my arrival. Maybe even crazy people are successful in combat, but I was concerned that this asshole was going to get a lot of good men killed. When we had Charlie on the run, Kellen wanted to take 12 troops and chase them into the jungle. Thankfully our Lieutenant stopped him. If allowed, Kellen was definitely going to get us all killed.

The second attack was more intense and we counter-attacked, chasing the enemy until they had no choice but to fight. I thought they fought pretty poorly and I quickly got over my fear.

It was a heated firefight and many of those sneaky buggers died. At the peak of the battle when it looked like they were going to be in full retreat, I found myself in a small ravine with six dead Viet Cong,

Sgt. Kellen and no one else. The battle was raging and the gunfire deafening, but in my immediate position, the firing from the enemy was such that I could keep myself out of harm's way and still return fire. Sgt. Kellen, on the other hand, was huddled behind a burnt out tree carcass, trembling with fear, while his soldiers were dodging bullets flying all around them.

My suspicions were confirmed about this sick bastard. He liked to beat people up and put them in the hospital, but when there was a chance he could be injured or killed, he all but crawled up into a fetal position. He was actually crying.

There was a dead VC three feet from me and no one else even close, so without a split second of thought, I took advantage of a golden opportunity. I picked up the Chinese M3 Grease Gun from the fallen VC and gave Sgt. Kellen a short burst. His eyes met mine at the exact moment I squeezed off the rounds, so he knew he was going to die. I didn't care.

When he went down, I dropped the enemy rifle, picked up my own and ran over to see if Kellen was dead. I knew before I got to him that he couldn't be alive with that many holes in him, so I hustled up the short distance to the north side of the ravine and quickly blended in with the others in my unit. The whole thing didn't take two minutes. If I was going to die here, it wouldn't be because of that piece of shit.

When the battle was over, we found that while we killed well over 300 VC, we had suffered almost 100 casualties ourselves. Of course, Sgt. Kellen was one of them. There were enough dead Viet-Cong soldiers nearby to make it obvious that he, along with all the other American casualties, had been killed by enemy fire. In the desperation of battle, with bullets flying around by the thousands, you are not watching other soldiers. You are too busy trying to keep yourself alive. No one had seen Kellen go down.

I was as cold as ice about it and didn't care a whit that he was probably given a hero's funeral and most likely a medal of honor. I never found out and never cared. All I knew was there was one less asshole in the world.

I also had a revelation about myself. After giving it a lot of thought and remembering all of the people I had killed up to that point, I realized I had run a lot of risks in the past. Risks of being caught, risks of being overpowered and perhaps killed, or worse, discovered when attempting to kill. These were all people who needed killing, but I still did not want to be caught or killed either, so this last action taught me two things. One was that I had to start being more careful and two, if I could do my killings with a gun, it would mean less danger to myself and it would make for an easier kill.

Suppose my kick to Beaver Shit's balls had missed? Suppose Kevin had been able to grab the hoe and pull me into the vat? I was seeing the light about just how fortunate I had been, but I also knew that my luck could quickly run out if I wasn't smarter. It made sense to stop counting on luck. I would be better served to prepare more for bad luck and how to handle that, should things go unexpectedly sour.

I decided that any future efforts to get rid of scumbags when I got back to the World would have to be approached with more care.

In no way did that decision include these little black-hearted fuckers in Vietnam. We killed these people on sight because they were going to do the same to us, given the chance. The hardest thing to understand was, they would sell you merchandise, shine your shoes, supply a girlfriend for the afternoon or some other service during the day with a smile on their face, and at night the same little shit who laughed with you over a drink, would sneak into your camp and cut your throat. We came to think of them as sub-humans. I know now that it was wrong but who said war was supposed to be right. When you have someone trying to kill you, you can't afford to ask why. You simply kill him first.

# 17

During the rest of my tour in Vietnam, there were many more battles and many more hills to take, only to abandon and re-take a month later. The reason for this was never explained to us and I sometimes wondered if anyone knew if there was one. It was like the entire war was being run by idiots at a war game board and we were the tiny toy soldiers. Many good people died in Vietnam for no valid reason, and too many more came home in pieces or without pieces.

I was one of the lucky ones who came home intact. Thankfully, I never got a scratch, but it left mental scars on just about everyone, including me. Many soldiers who came home with their bodies intact had their heads fucked up. Some of them came home with drug habits picked up over there and needed rehab, and others were just messed up from the horrors of war.

You can't be teasing your buddy about his girl back home one minute, and see him lying next to you with a hole in his head the next, without experiencing some form of emotional damage. The horrors that came from combat bothered me, but not as much as some. I grieved for the American boys being killed but I was firm in my convictions that these deadly little pajama clad buggers needed killing. So I killed as many of them as I could. Oddly, I never was afraid of being killed myself. It was like fighting children who had no training in combat, so I was not in the least bit frightened by them. Go figure.

I finally came home after my tour was done, if you can call flying into San Francisco home. I quickly decided that I was not going to go to Arizona on my leave. Instead, I went to New Orleans. I thought the women might be easier there and that was what I needed. There were plenty of hookers in Vietnam and I partook of my share, but I was never terribly enamored with them because they were so small, it almost felt like you were having sex with children. I think Kevin would have loved it.

New Orleans had liquor flowing down the streets and plenty of willing women, but I soon found out that if you wandered anywhere away from the main drags, it was as seamy as any other inner city, with someone looking to rob or kill you on every corner. I spent a few days there and then left on a plane to Los Angeles.

I spent the rest of my leave in LA, shacked up with a girl I knew from high school, in the short time I had spent there. She lived in a suburb of Los Angeles and she was pretty loose about our relationship, with no expectations. I was good with staying there for the week of freedom remaining on my leave.

The rest of my Army hitch was spent greasing and assembling tank tracks in a motor pool at Ft Dix, New Jersey. It was a dull fourteen months after the fever pitch of battle in Vietnam.

When my Military Obligation was fulfilled and I was finally discharged, I made a beeline for LA, but the girl I stayed with when on leave had moved away and left no forwarding address. For all I knew, she could be married with a kid by now. I wasn't too disappointed because I wasn't looking to marry her. I simply wanted a warm, familiar body to take the edge off.

I rented a room in what must have once been a hotel in another of the many suburbs of Los Angeles and spent some time just hanging around, enjoying not having to wear a uniform. I knew that sooner or later, I was going to have to get a job. I had saved a decent sum of money when I was an enlisted man, but money can be spent fast once you're back in civilian life.

Not being a drug user or one to party with booze, drugs and women, I found when I was enlisted, that I didn't need much to live on, so I loaned money to other soldiers who had habits or gambled and usually spent their pay long before the paymaster came around again. I made short-term loans at a decent and profitable interest rate and saved all of it while I was there. The borrowers would always pay me as soon as they got paid, because they knew they would be broke again by the middle of the month. Staying on my good side meant the difference between having fun in the second half of the month and spending their spare time at the Enlisted Men's Club, playing ping-pong. I occasionally had someone try to cheat me but they always met with an unfortunate accident that made them reconsider their actions. It seldom happened twice. I suppose one could have called me a loan shark, but at that time, I didn't know or care much about loan sharking.

I preferred to think of myself as a soldier helping my fellow soldiers while helping myself as well. I was simply providing a service, albeit a profitable one.

So, here I was in LA with enough money to last a good long while, but still knowing I was going to have to do something sooner or later to keep my cushion well padded. In my first week there, I did two important things. I bought a seven-year-old Ford and a .45 caliber Colt from a guy I knew who got it from a guy, through a guy who knew a guy. If Vietnam had taught me nothing else, it taught me that if someone needed killing it was much smarter to do it from a distance. I was a pretty tough ex-soldier, but I shouldn't take those kinds of chances if I didn't have to. I didn't want to find my name in the Obituaries any time soon. Nor did I want to find it on any Police Department's crime sheet.

The first thing I had to decide was, what was I good at? Lubricating tracks on tanks? I didn't think so. The only thing I seemed to be good at was killing people. Thinking about it and reflecting on what I had been doing for most of my life was a little chilling. I wasn't fearful of killing, but I didn't intend to be a random killer either.

If I ever had to kill anyone again, like in my life before Vietnam, any potential victim would have to be someone who was a clear threat to me. I didn't consider the Viet Cong as kills because they were faceless people in a senseless war. I pointed my rifle and shot, not really caring who or how many I killed as long as I got them before they got me, so I never let emotions enter the equation.

If there was a way to make money killing people who needed killing, I could almost be happy with that, but I wasn't really about searching out bad people to kill. I was not going to mess with Mafia people or anything like that either, because once you get them on your tail you might as well eat your gun yourself. They will get you sooner or later and kill you with no more thought than they would give to swatting a bug. I have never seen an old retired killer of Mafia hit men sitting in a rocking chair.

I heard it said that every time a soldier kills, a little bit of himself dies too. Having greased my share of the enemy in Vietnam and having gotten rid of a few monsters right here in the World, I didn't agree with that at all. I did what I had to do in all of those cases with no regrets. In fact, I was happy I killed the people I had to kill. Considering the evil in them and who they would have gone on to hurt if I hadn't come along, not a bit of me died with them.

After a few weeks of staying in the place I used for a room, I heard from a guy I served with in Vietnam, who rotated out before me and was discharged ahead of me. He was working in a factory on the east coast where they manufactured radial airplane engines for bombers for the Government. He assured me that he could get me a job if I wanted to go back there. After thinking about it for a day, I called him back, got a few more details, and decided it was a no-brainer. I pointed the nose of my Ford east on I-40 and headed for the other side of the country.

# 18

I arrived in Connecticut in just five days and two days later, I was hired for the job in Hartford, as promised. It turned out the foreman in my department was a Vietnam Vet himself and was more than happy to give Veterans like myself priority in his hiring. It paid quite well and there were plenty of opportunities for overtime because the war in Vietnam was far from over. Our planes were still being shot down every day. My job was assembling pistons and connecting rods for twelve-cylinder airplane engines. It was a simple, but important procedure. I was happy to have something to do every day and even happier to get a good paycheck.

I bunked on my friend's sofa for three weeks, then bought a practically new, sixty-five foot double-wide mobile home in a decent, but hardly posh mobile home park. The homes were spaced over fifty feet apart and well shaded by shrubbery and trees.

Unlike some parks where the coaches are packed like sardines, this afforded me all the privacy I wanted.

It was in a small town northwest of Hartford, called Lost River. Whoever named the town had a sense of humor, because the joke was, there was no river. It was a little under a twenty minute drive to work on a narrow, tree-lined road. My mobile home wasn't anything fancy, but it was very well made. It had modern appliances and was much nicer than what we expect to see in trailer parks.

The original owner bought it after her husband passed away, planning to live out her final years there, but unfortunately, shortly after set-up she suffered a stroke while at the grocery store. She died the next day in the hospital after living in her new home for just a week.

I had no intention of retiring there, thinking more along the lines of staying only as long as it took to save enough to hit the road for a few years. Buying made more sense than paying rent for a house or apartment and it definitely beat sleeping on somebody's couch, on someone's floor or in my car. I knew even while I was still in the Army that I wouldn't be content staying in any one place for very long. Maybe a little of the wanderlust came from the moving around we did when I was a kid.

My new mobile home was bigger than a self-professed loner like me needed, but I thought the extra space wouldn't hurt. When I decided to move on, I thought I could easily sell it for more than I paid for it. Besides, just paying rent somewhere always seemed like flushing money down the toilet. There was a space rental fee, but it was only thirty-five dollars a month and it included lawn care, trash pickup and snow removal in winter.

Just when you think you are getting your life sorted out and think you know where you will be in a few months or years, life comes up and hits you in the face. It often happens when you least expect it.

It slapped me hard one day at work, when I met a girl who inspected small electric motor parts in the department next to mine. She captured my interest the moment I saw her. I found out through asking around that her name was Stella Wilson, and like me, she was single. In spite of my desire to be happy as a loner, I thought no harm would be done by looking, so I watched her from afar for a time before I spoke with her. You can learn a lot about someone by simply observing them from a distance.

Stella was about 5'2," probably weighed one-fifteen and while she wasn't the drop-dead kind of gorgeous, she was gorgeous in a quiet sort of way. She could elicit looks and second looks, but wasn't necessarily a girl who would be ogled, because she just didn't display that kind of appearance. She had shoulder length dark brown hair, not straight, but with a little flair, and she had puffy bangs. She had sultry brown eyes you could get lost in.

She wasn't very tall, but had a willowy appearance with a limber, athletic look. She was slim of hip, leggy, with a small waist and firm, adequate breasts, not small, but not huge. She carried herself with good posture while not looking stiff and when she walked, she had just the slightest hint of swagger in an otherwise unassuming gait. I could look at her all day.

She dressed conservatively, but if you had eyes you could tell she had a killer body. She had a confidence in her looks that didn't require an effort to look sexy. At least not to me. She didn't need heavy makeup or to show a lot of skin to make herself stand out. There was a classy look about her that told you she would never stoop to drinking beer out of a can, but wouldn't frown on others for doing it. I couldn't take my freaking eyes off her.

One day at lunch, I saw her alone at the food truck, so I skillfully made my way over to her. She was trying to choose between what was being passed off as a roast beef sandwich and a tuna melt. They both looked like expired leftovers from my refrigerator.

I quietly watched her for a minute and took in her good looks while she thought over which sandwich she would chance. I tried for my best Jack Kennedy smile and said, "You know, either one of these could kill you in about 30 minutes."

She smiled back at me and said, "Well, everybody has to die from something."

Her smile could have lit up the world's darkest room. I hadn't seen her smile before and now having it directed at me, I was melting like ice cream in the hot August sun. Her lightly tanned face showed spirit and intelligence, with the slightest hint of mischief, and her lips were just asking to be kissed.

My limited experience with women left me a bit short in my repertoire of come-backs, so I think I said something about what a shame it would be to die at work. After I said it, I wanted to hide somewhere because it must have sounded pretty juvenile. Stella only laughed.

We introduced ourselves and made small talk for a few minutes. Close up, her tiny frame looked strong, yet soft at the same time. I might be a self-professed loner, but at that moment, she made me feel more alive than I had been in a very long time.

It was like suddenly turning on a bright light in a place that had been dark for too long. Stella had just enough of everything in all the right places to make her ever so easy on the eyes. Talking with her made me feel like I was a teenager again. It was so excitingly unexpected, I had to force myself to concentrate and get a grip on my emotions. So far, I probably wasn't making a very good impression.

Very quickly, it was time to go back to work, but I didn't want my time with her to be over this soon. I asked her to have dinner with me if she didn't already have plans. She said she did have plans, but thanked me for asking. My disappointment must have been obvious, because as she walked away, she turned back to me, smiled and said, "Ask me again tomorrow." And in the blink of an eye she was gone.

I spent my evening alone, downed a couple of cocktails and thought about her and what she might be doing. Surprisingly, I found myself jealous that she could be on a date with some jerkoff who probably didn't have honorable intentions. It was riding me hard. I barely knew her and here I was with my boxers in a knot about who she might or might not be with. As the saying goes, I didn't know whether to shit or wind my watch.

Wouldn't you know it, the next day she didn't come to work. What kind of luck was this? Now I was really in a bad way, but there was nothing I could do. I didn't even have her phone number. If I did, I would have called and made a fool out of myself, so it was probably a good thing I couldn't do that. All I could do was try to keep my mind on my work and not screw up an engine. I hated to think some poor bastard in Southeast Asia could die because I was a pouting Mr. Lonely today.

A few days ago, I didn't even know her, was a happy, self-professed loner, destined to be one forever, and here I was, less than a week later, so smitten that I couldn't put a square peg in a square hole. I was tripping over my own feet.

The next day was Wednesday and when I went outside for lunch, there she was. I ambled over, trying not to look too eager and said, "I missed you yesterday."

She smiled that winning smile and said, "I had some family business that needed my attention."

Then she said, "Sorry I wasn't around to see you the other night. But I am free tonight if that offer is still open."

I said it was and asked her what kind of food she liked besides the poison from the food truck. She laughed and said she was just a Plain Jane pizza girl. I told her she was anything but a Plain Jane and asked where I could pick her up. She surprised me by saying she would meet me at the Pizza Barn out on the State Highway. She assured me it was just about the only place in Lost River to get a good pizza.

That evening when I got there, she was already seated at a table outside, looking like a girl who might be waiting for someone. It put a noticeable spring in my step, knowing that someone was me.

Unlike the dull clothes I saw her in at work, she now wore shorts, a pink blouse, and sneakers. Her brown hair moving with the breeze just added to her desirability. I was struck dumb by just what a fine looking woman she was. Stella seemed like she was glowing and right then she could have reached into my chest and pulled out my heart. I didn't know what was happening, but I liked it. With the events unfolding around me like they were for almost all of my life, I had always kept girls at arm's length, telling myself that things couldn't work out because of my history. I never wanted to start something that I would only lose when things inevitably went south. This surprise infatuation was puzzling, and it felt mighty damn good.

It didn't look to me like she was wearing anything under her blouse and from my vantage point the scenery was delicious.

A teenaged waitress with enough hardware in her mouth to build a Buick came to take our order. Suffering from dry mouth and a total loss of focus, I asked the waitress to give us a few minutes. Then I felt like a dope because, after all, we were just at a pizza place wanting to have some pizza.

How hard could that be?

If Stella noticed my regression to adolescence and my inability to walk and talk at the same time, she never let on, but I was embarrassing myself. Guys were supposed to be smooth, cool and unflappable, but tonight you would think I was a tongue-tied, country bumpkin in the presence of a movie star. Maybe star- struck would be a good way to describe my night so far.

It was time to hunker down and get back on track.

We chatted until the waitress with the metal mouth returned and took our order, which, after all that, was just pizza and beer.

We ate and we laughed and we drank and we laughed and time seemed to fly by. We had enough to drink so neither of us was feeling much pain and by the time we tore ourselves away from each other, we saw that the Pizza Barn was almost empty. It was already eleven o'clock.

I didn't want the night to end, but we both had to go to work in the morning. She was the first one to speak and said that we needed to call it a night. When I asked when I could see her again, she slyly looked at me and questioned, "When do you want to see me again?"

Being the Casanova that I was, I said, "How about tomorrow morning when I open my eyes?"

To my delight, she didn't get all squirrelly, but instead replied, "Maybe a little bit slower, Cowboy." Then she giggled, kissed my cheek, slid away from me and was gone.

For the next three or four days Stella and I met at the Roach Coach at break time and had our lunches together in the designated area outdoors. We kept the conversation light, although I asked to see her again every day. Every day she gave me her winning smile, saying she had some family business to attend to. In our second week of this, she said yes, but asked if we could make it on the weekend.

That Friday, at lunch, when I pointed out that the weekend was upon us, she suggested eating again at the Pizza Barn. I happily accepted, although I was thinking more like a drive-in movie. This time, she said I could pick her up at her place at about seven. She said she lived closer to work than I did, still on the outskirts of Hartford, which wasn't much of a drive.

The rest of the day dragged like I was winning a million dollars but not until the end of my shift.

Eventually the work day did end and I hurried home to shower and change. I didn't want to be late.

The confusion over my feelings was still a nagging problem in my mind. I knew I couldn't have a relationship with Stella and I certainly couldn't let her know my history, yet she thrilled me in a way that wouldn't let me slow myself down. She simply made me feel good. I decided I would live for today and deal with tomorrow's problems tomorrow. Besides, I didn't have any indication that she was as swept away as me, so I was probably reading more into this than I should. To her, it might be just another pizza.

Stella lived in a little bungalow not far off the state road, and when I knocked on her door, she opened it and once again took my breath away. Just when I thought she couldn't look any better. She had her hair pinned up and you could see where her neck was still damp from a shower. I could also tell without a doubt that underneath a still conservative looking yellow, sleeveless top, there was no bra. She was wearing jeans that fit like she was made specifically for them and with the sneakers she wore, she could have been off to a Fifties Sock Hop.

I politely asked, "Is your mother at home?"

She laughed with her infectious laugh and said, "No she isn't. Will I do?"

I replied, "You surely will!" And she laughed again.

So, it was off to the Pizza Barn, where I did a great job of making conversation. It was hard to do, when all I really wanted to do was ravish her until the sun came up. They say that a man can't think straight when he has lust in his soul and that may be true, but I was giving it my best shot anyway.

We were served again by the waitress with all the hardware and we ordered the same standard junk food that would make us both fat if this was a steady diet.

When the pizza came, we picked at it, like two teenagers on a first date. While we were still laughing at each other's wit, it became clear to me that we were both thinking about something besides a greasy pizza.

After a half hour of going through the motions with the pizza, she leaned close, gave me a shy look and whispered, "So what do you like for breakfast?"

We almost sprinted out of the Pizza Barn, piled into my Ford and broke all the speed limits to my castle in the park.

We barely got the door closed before we embraced with a kiss like I had never experienced before. It was an embrace that I never wanted to end. We clung to each other like wild animals, kissing and clawing at each other's clothes with a hunger so urgent that if lightning struck, neither of us would have noticed.

She wasn't wearing anything under the jeans either.

# 19

The next morning we awoke with a start, on the verge of panic, thinking we were late for work. Then we remembered it was Saturday. After that it took only a few moments of small talk, nibbling and touching and like magic, we were back into each other's arms. Her skin on my skin felt as good as anything I had experienced in a long while. It was closer to lunch time than breakfast before we gave any serious thought to food.

When the lovemaking finally slowed to a pace to allow some recovery time, we got down to talking, as lovers do after the release of so much passion. It's usually the time you begin telling each other the more intimate things you really don't know about each other, besides sex. Of course, in my case, pillow talk could get me in hot water. I tried to keep the conversation on a generic level because I was afraid if I ever told her about the real me, she would probably run out screaming. I didn't want to take any chance of ruining what was shaping up to be one hell of a weekend. At this point I was as vague as I could be about revealing too much of my past. I limited it to generic family stories and past places I lived before coming to Connecticut. I didn't think I would ever be able to tell her about the bad things, and really didn't want to think about it. If I was ever going to tell her, it would be far down the line into the distant future, if we had a future. I put it out of my mind for now because it was too early to be thinking about sharing revelations as serious as those. If it turned out we became a genuine item and our relationship demanded the truth, I would cross that bridge when I came to it.

Stella was also very reserved about herself, only sharing that she lived alone, after having lived for quite some time with her sister. She wasn't specific, but said she did have family obligations and would most likely not be available every night. She evidently felt my disappointment because she playfully poked me and said not to worry, she wasn't seeing anyone besides me. I wondered if she sensed as much as I did that we were both being vague. I sensed her reluctance to be too open, but it was far too early in our relationship to worry about it, so I didn't. I just savored the moment.

I told her about all the places I had lived, including Huckleberry Finn Town, which made her laugh. She thought all that moving was an unfortunate thing for me as a child. She hadn't lived in nearly as many places as me, but she understood better when I explained that moving around so much was a result of my dad's job transfers. She spoke very little about her family and I didn't press it. She would tell me when she wanted to.

I showed her the rest of my mobile home, which, thankfully was clean and presentable. She was impressed that a guy could live alone and not be a slob. Well, not too much of a slob.

While showing her around, she picked up the Colt .45 I had left on the kitchen counter, next to my breakfast cereal. She saw it when she went to start the coffee maker and said she liked guns. She picked it up, took the magazine out and ejected the round from the chamber before inspecting it further. I was surprised to see that this little girl knew her way around guns. In my experience, most girls didn't like guns and were afraid of them. Stella handled it like she was born with it. I was becoming more impressed by the minute with this unique woman.

We eventually had to get dressed, so we did, and spent the day together, just trying to get to know each other. Happily, the clothes were off a few more times before I took her home. When we said goodbye, she shared her wish to see more of me than just having lunch together at work or an occasional greasy pizza. I agreed that my feelings were the same.

My infatuation with Stella, if that's what it was, set off a warning buzzer in my head because everything was happening so fast. The startling effect she had on me in such a short time caused terribly conflicting thoughts. I was so sure there couldn't be a woman in my life, at least not for a long time, yet here I was, acting like a brain-dead, hormonal teenager.

I didn't want to be emotionally involved with anyone until I was sure my other life was far behind me, and would never cause a problem. Until it was, a relationship like the one into which I was heading would be destined to fail. I was afraid that being deeply in love with any woman could cloud my judgment if I was ever forced to take the law into my own hands again. And clouded judgement usually ends badly.

I never knew if or when my past would catch up with me and make me disappear in a hurry. If, by chance someone from Michigan, Arizona or even the Army put two and two together, the jig could be up.

Going to prison doesn't do much to cement a relationship, nor does disappearing. I wondered what Stella's reaction would be if she learned the truth about my adventures. Would she run away like a sensible woman should or could I explain things so she would understand? I was afraid to become emotionally attached, so although I desperately wanted to continue seeing her, I had to be mindful of her innocence and strive to keep her that way. I hated lying to her, but telling her my story wasn't in the cards right now. How to control what I felt when I was with her was the problem. When she was there, I didn't care about another thing in the world besides the moment.

Stella and I began seeing each other almost every night, although we kept it under wraps for a while at work for fear of the inevitable gossip affecting our workplaces. We didn't want anything to jeopardize our relationship.

Then one day when I saw her at the "roach coach" I could tell she was in distress and appeared unreachable. When I asked her what was wrong, she shook her head and said it was nothing that involved me, but said she needed some space. That was a jolt. Everything was pointing to an increasingly happy relationship and now she needed "space"? It was my experience that "space" was something you asked for when it was over and you hadn't come up with a way to tell the person being dumped that it's over. Unable to help and unable to understand, I agreed to cool off for a little, and wait for a signal from her that whatever it was, was past.

I didn't see Stella for a few days, either at work or at night, and she wasn't answering her phone. I didn't know what to think. At first I thought she was sick, but if she was sick, I was sure she would call me.

No matter how I tried, I couldn't imagine why she suddenly disappeared. I thought we had a good thing going, but I guessed I must have been mistaken. It wouldn't be the first time for me and probably wouldn't be the last. I was heartbroken to think she might be seeing someone else. It was a harsh curveball, because I thought we were becoming so close. I had fallen so hard in such a short time that I couldn't believe it was gone, just like that. Once again, my limited relationships with girls kept me from knowing what to do. I had so much to learn.

I experienced the disbelief, denial, anger and grief, but none of it helped. I guessed it was over.

Then, although my better judgment was screaming at me not to, I started watching Stella's house after work. I suppose one could call it stalking.

For four nights I parked out of sight and watched her place through binoculars until well after midnight, but there was no sign of her. I couldn't imagine where she could be or why she had shut me out, but evidently she was away somewhere and didn't appear to be coming home. Did this mean she had a new boyfriend with whom she was staying? I just couldn't accept that I had been dumped.

On the fifth night of my stake-out, I got to Stella's while it was still daylight and her Malibu was parked in front where it usually is. I was tempted to knock on the door, but thought perhaps I should wait it out a little while and see if I could find out what was happening. I didn't want to walk in and find her with some other guy because I didn't know what I would do in that scenario. I knew we were in the very early stage of a relationship, but as infatuated as I was, it would have hurt badly, so at least this once, common sense prevailed and I waited.

At about 10 o'clock, Stella came out of her house alone and got in her car. She sat there for a few minutes before driving away. When she did, I followed her.

She drove carefully, within the speed limits for about seven miles, until she was on the outskirts of town in a warehouse district. I stayed a safe distance behind, hoping she wouldn't spot me. I didn't want to arouse her suspicions. When she turned into a driveway in the middle of a warehouse complex, I stopped well back from where she turned in and parked behind a building on the other side of the street, where my car couldn't be seen. I followed from there on foot. There was no other way out of the yard, so if she turned around and left, she would have to pass right by me. I had a very bad feeling about this from the get-go, so when I left my car, I took a baseball bat out of my trunk, glad that I had kept it in there. I hoped this was innocent, but people don't go into deserted places like this in the dark of night for something innocent. I had enough experience with bad things that I could smell a dangerous situation from a mile away. I was sure this was one of them.

After I passed a few buildings, I began to hear a hysterical woman's voice. It sounded like Stella and she was loudly screaming at someone. I couldn't make out the words, but the tone indicated they weren't pleasant. I heard an occasional man's voice trying to get a word in edgewise and being cut off by Stella's screaming. I wished I had brought my .45 instead of a baseball bat, and made a mental note to never leave home without it again. I ran to the door at the end of the metal building where the yelling was coming from, and peeked inside.

I wasn't prepared for what I saw.

# 20

A heavy-set balding man wearing a cheap brown suit was on his knees, with his hands clasped on top of his head, in what was an otherwise empty warehouse. Stella was standing ten feet in front of him, holding a 9mm Beretta pointed at his very red face.

After a second to take in what I was seeing, I shouted, "Stella!"

She looked at me with shock on her face, but her gun hand never wavered.

I asked her, "Who is he and what are you doing?"

Stella said, "Chris, you need to stay out of this! This is between him and me!"

The balding fat man cried out, "You have to help me! This crazy bitch is trying to kill me!"

I asked Stella to put the gun down and talk to me. At first she refused, but after gentle coaxing from me, she finally lowered the gun just a little. It was still pointed in the fat man's general direction, so he knew better than to move a muscle.

I spoke softly and asked Stella what was going on.

She said, "This son of a bitch killed my sister and I'm not going to let him get away with it."

Confused, I tried to make some sense of what she was saying. She had told me she used to live with her sister, but she never said anything about her sister being dead, let alone murdered. I had no way of making sense of any of this, but knew I needed to try to cool Stella's anger long enough to give me time to figure out what to do.

I said, "If he killed your sister, shouldn't we call the Police and report it?"

She took a few deep breaths and explained, pointing to fat boy, "You don't understand. This is what he does. He works for the mob and all he does is kill people."

I mulled this over for a few seconds and asked, "What does this have to do with you?"

She answered, "My father got into trouble with loan sharks a few years ago and disappeared to stay alive. When they couldn't find him, they came to my sister and me, hoping to find him through us. We didn't know where he was, so they threatened me and my sister, trying to make us tell them where my father was hiding. They didn't believe we didn't know where he was, so they sent this motherfucker to kill us. In my sister's case, he succeeded."

I asked the guy, "What do you have to say to all of this?"

He replied in a shaky voice, "This girl is crazy. She made this whole story up! Please take the gun away from her!"

Stella screamed, "You're a fucking liar! You only agreed to meet me here because I said I would bring the money that my father owed. I'm not stupid. I know you would have just killed me afterward, even if I had it!"

She continued to me, "But I'm smarter than he thought. I set this up to get even with him and he walked right into it."

I looked at the guy and his face gave him away. Stella was telling the truth. I needed to act quickly or this was going to get out of control fast. If Stella shot him here, the gunfire would be heard and it wouldn't be good to be near this area.

I carefully said, "Stella, I need you to back up and point your gun away from him so I can talk with him for a minute. The look she gave me said she wasn't going to do that.

I asked her if she trusted me. She looked like she was on the edge of her sanity, so I fervently promised it would be alright and that I knew what I was doing.

She hesitated for a minute, looked at me like she really wished I had not interrupted, then backed up a couple of steps.

I swiftly stepped into that space she left between her and the fat guy. I got a look of tremendous relief from him just before I whacked him behind the ear with the end of my baseball bat.

He collapsed to the floor, unconscious. I quickly checked him and found a pistol in a belt holster behind his back. It was only a .380, but it was big enough to get the job done that he evidently came here to do.

I turned to Stella, who was clearly on the verge of panic, and asked if her car was parked nearby. Taking her gaze from his supine form on the floor, she looked at me and said "Yes."

I told her to go get it right away, drive it over to the side door and for heaven's sake, put the Beretta away before someone saw her with it.

She asked, "Where did you come from and why did you stop me?"

I replied, "I love you and I believe in you, but this isn't the place for this. Please go get your car."

She turned and left without a word.

While she was getting her car, I removed the killer's shoelaces and tied his wrists tightly behind his back with them. I stuffed his handkerchief into his mouth and wrapped his well-stretched leather belt over his mouth to keep it in place.

I dragged him to the door by his feet, looked out and saw a three-year-old Mercury parked outside of the other door. Assuming it was his, I searched his pockets, found keys and luckily, one of them opened the trunk of the Mercury. When Stella came back, I asked her to help me, and we struggled to pile his fat ass into the trunk of his car.

Stella asked, "Why did you have me go get my car if we're going to take him out of here in the trunk of his own car?"

The answer to this was obvious, but she wouldn't be receptive to any explanation right now. Sending her to get her car was the best way to get her cooled off while I figured out what to do next. I didn't want anyone in a panic trying to make decisions, and Stella was in full panic mode. Going to get her car just gave her something to do and removed her from the situation for a few minutes, giving me time to decide what our next step was.

Rather than tell her the truth, I said, "I changed my mind. I decided it would be better if he was never in your car."

That seemed to momentarily make sense to her. She took a minute to regain her composure and asked, "So what now?"

I said, "We need to get him away from here."

"There's a dirt road about four miles away, right off this street, just beyond the water tower on the right. Follow me there. When I stop at the water tower, leave your car on the blacktop behind the pumping station where it can't be seen and come get in this car with me."

Stella nodded, with an wide-eyed expression, which told me she was still excited and adrenaline was continuing to control her, but she abruptly turned and got in her Malibu.

My car was parked in another lot, where no one could see it, so that wasn't a concern. We could come back and get it later. I drove the Mercury with the fat guy in the trunk, obeying the speed limit, seeming to be in no hurry, although I was still afraid of being seen. I was just coming into this whole shit storm and didn't know who, if anyone, would recognize his car, remember seeing it or wonder why I was driving it.

When we came to the water tower, I stopped beside it while Stella drove her car around to the back. She got in the Mercury and we followed the dirt road in silence until we came to a turnoff, where I slowly turned in. We drove about a hundred yards, deep into the woods bordering the dirt road. It was overgrown and looked like no one had traveled it in quite some time. I had been told once that there used to be a Nudist Camp in this area that closed over a decade ago, so I didn't expect to run into anyone. I hoped it hadn't become a lover's lane, but not seeing tracks of any kind, I relaxed a little.

Once we stopped, it was time for me to find out what was going on. I asked Stella what she had been going to do and to tell me again, why.

Calmed down somewhat, she replied, "I was going to blow his fucking brains out."

I again asked her to explain. She said, "He deserves to die for killing my sister. If I hadn't pulled my gun first in that warehouse, he would have killed me too. You see, he has to die for me to be safe."

I asked, "Have you ever done this before?"

After a long, defensive look, she answered, "What if I have?'

I said, "I think we need to talk for a moment before we do something we can't change. Do you understand the magnitude of killing someone? Do you know that it could haunt you for the rest of your life?"

She confidently said, "I can handle it."

We were in a place which was completely deserted yet not too far off the main road. I had stopped beside the dirt path in a field of grass on purpose so there would be no evidence of shoe prints or anything else traceable.

I looked at Stella and said, "Do you really have to do this?"

She said, "I didn't ask for your help and I'm not asking you to get involved any further, so if you want to leave, just go back to my car and wait for me. I'll be there in a few minutes."

I told her that I was in this to stay, but I needed some facts.

She laid out the whole story for me.

It seems her father was once connected and worked either for or with the mob. He was involved in loan sharking for some high rollers and he had either gambled away money that wasn't his, lost it or stole it and couldn't pay his bosses. Knowing what would happen to him, he dropped out of sight.

When the Mob couldn't find him, they sent their henchman to harass his daughters and threaten them, trying to make them give up their father's whereabouts. The problem was, Stella and her sister, Patty, didn't know where their father was. They hadn't seen him in years. Their father left their mother when they were quite young and they hadn't heard from him since. They were completely unaware of his mob ties or any gambling problem. Having had no contact with him and no idea where he was, naturally they couldn't be of any help, but mob people don't always believe the first story they get, even if it's the truth.

Then one night, they sent an enforcer, our guy in the trunk, to their house while Patty was home alone. He beat her, raped her and then beat her some more. Stella knew who did it, because although she had been out at the time of the attack, just as she was returning home, she saw this fat, balding guy running out of the house. She knew him from a time when he had threatened them before, so she easily recognized him running from the scene.

She ran into the house and found her sister beaten, raped and dead.

Stella and her sister had reported the harassment once to the local law enforcement, but there was never any Police action taken. Now that there was a murder that appeared to be mob related, the FBI came into the picture. They didn't close the case, because they were never able to find her sister's killer. They should have known it wouldn't end there. Stella was still getting threats, so they wanted to put her into the Witness Protection Program. She resisted doing it at first, but events happened that changed her mind. It was hard to understand, with all that had taken place, how the authorities were not able to find Patty's killer.

Stella explained to me how the Witness Protection Program works. They moved her away, leaving no word for any friends or relatives to use to contact her.

They gave her a new identity, new Social Security number, new credit lines and got her a job working where we met. She could have no contact at all with any family or friends until this was over, if then. The old Stella had dropped out of sight. It wasn't supposed to be a permanent thing, only until her sister's murderer was caught and they could be sure she was no longer in danger.

I asked her how they would ever determine that, knowing it was a stupid question. The mob would only leave her alone if and when they located her father or got their money and maybe not even then because she knew too much. As for Stella's father, he was a dead duck no matter what. If he somehow managed to pay back his debt to the mob, they would still make an example of him. They couldn't show any hint of forgiveness because it would be interpreted as weakness. Weakness was something they could never show for obvious reasons.

This had kept them from finding Stella, but it had not stopped Stella from finding this son of a bitch we had in the trunk.

She explained that when she was telling me she had family business to take care of, she was working with a couple of contacts from her other life, tracking down the scumbag who killed her sister. She contacted a man who knew her father and who evidently knew of his connection. He gave her information that she took to another man who worked for the Protection Program. The Program guy was able to use the information Stella had from her father's old friend.

Between her persistence and his digging, she found where her sister's killer was and she was eventually able to get a telephone number to contact him, which is how she worked out this deal.

So, here we were, in a volatile situation with a man in the trunk. Stella would be in trouble with her witness protection people if they found out what she was doing because it could blow the covers of other people as well as her own, if her persistence backfired. The mob is quite unforgiving.

When she found him and contacted him, his eager cooperation soon told her he was going to work alone.

She was sure he wouldn't go to his bosses and tell them she contacted him. He was undoubtedly planning to take the money, kill her and keep the money for himself. Once he disposed of her body, his bosses would never know and he would be a rich man.

After much negotiating over how and where she would complete the payoff, she managed to lure him to the warehouse, promising to pay her father's debt in full. He agreed to meet her and when he came alone, her suspicions were confirmed. Of course, she was counting on this. If he had come with reinforcements, she would wind up as dead as her sister. She took a hell of a chance, but in this case her instincts were good. He was going to pocket the money and put a bullet in her head, so she could never tell anyone. Unfortunately for the killer, he had underestimated Stella, and let her get the drop on him. Now he had no one to help him. No one ever said mob enforcers were Einsteins.

Listening to her story, I knew she was telling the truth. You can't make this stuff up.

I asked her, "So what do you want to do?"

She replied, "There is only one thing I can do to keep this asshole from killing me like he killed my sister. What would you do?"

There was only one answer to that.

We found a rag under the front seat of the Mercury and used it to wipe down everything we had touched, leaving no prints. I again brandished my solid ash baseball bat and walked to the back of the car.

When I opened the trunk, the killer had regained consciousness and was struggling with his bindings. He had almost freed himself, but "almost" only counts in horse-shoes and hand grenades He stopped struggling when I opened the lid.

Stella stuck her face close to his and said, "You'll never rape or kill another girl, motherfucker!"

He began to shake his head in denial, but you could see, as you can with most cowards, that he knew why all of this was happening. Then, being the dumb bastard that he was, he gave Stella a defiant look. It was his last mistake.

She shot him in the eye.

# 21

There was no question that fat boy was dead. A 9mm jacketed hollow point can make a hell of a mess and this was no exception. Thankfully the blood, bone and brain splatter was limited to the deep end of the trunk and it didn't appear either of us had any of the mess on us.

I searched his pockets and found his wallet which contained a little over three hundred dollars, a Texaco credit card and a Pennsylvania Driver's License identifying him as George Howard Trafta. He was forty-four years old and not going to get any older.

I kept the wallet and shut the trunk, wishing I had a can of gasoline and a few matches. I didn't, so setting the car on fire was not an option. I took Stella's arm and said "Let's get the fuck out of here."

We quickly ran the distance back to her car, being careful to stay on grass, so we wouldn't leave any footprints, Stella jumped in the driver's side and when there was no traffic on the road, we left the scene. She had parked on blacktop, leaving no tire marks, so nothing could trace this back to us.

We didn't speak about the dead guy we had left in the trunk. Instead of having that discussion now, we talked about how sure we were about not leaving tracks in the woods or at the warehouse.

It was then we remembered my car was still in the warehouse district, so we drove back to retrieve it. When we arrived, we sat in silence for a few minutes, our eyes searching for anything out of place. We still couldn't be sure Fat Boy didn't have back-up.

After ten minutes passed, seeing nothing moving, there appeared no reason to suspect any danger, so I went to my car and let myself in. Before I did, we agreed to meet immediately at my house. Stella was still running on adrenalin and needed to come down. When she did, she would crash and I thought it better for her to crash at my place than at a stoplight somewhere.

# 22

Thankfully no one saw us return to the Trailer Park. Once we were inside, with the door closed behind us, I asked Stella if she knew what she had just done.

She looked back at me and said, "Yes, I just killed a fucking asshole."

I made drinks and we sat on the sofa and took a few deep breaths. We knew it was time to get it all out, but neither of us knew where to start or who should begin.

Stella finally broke the silence, saying, "I know this is going to make things different between us, but I have a confession to make. You asked me if I knew what killing someone felt like. I have done this before and with the mob still looking for me, I may have to do it again, so if you can't live with that, I may as well leave right now."

Completely taken by surprise, I asked, "What do you mean?"

She said, "Just that. I won't stay around and fuck up your life with troubles from my past. I'm sorry for not telling you any of this before, but there was a lot to tell. I haven't had what you would call a normal life and I'm sorry for getting you involved in something this bizarre. If you want me to go away, I'll go right now. There's no reason to drag this out."

I answered, "Stella, you're the best thing that's ever happened to me. I doubt you could tell me anything that would drive me away. If you think something would, please tell me about it and let me decide. We've got time and I need to know. There isn't anything that you can't tell me, so get it off your chest."

I continued, "I'll listen to anything you have to say and then I'll take the floor because I have a few things to tell you too. This is a good time for us to clear the air. I don't want to lose you."

She looked into my eyes for a minute and said, "You told me in that warehouse that you love me. Well, I love you too. I don't want to lose you either, but I have to tell you a few things about me that may be worse than you think."

When I didn't reply, she began, "There have been a few other times when I've had to kill somebody in order to protect myself. I'm not proud of that, but I did what I had to do."

Again she paused to see my reaction.

Getting none, she began her story. "The first time I was just a senior in high school, taking lessons in playing the flute. My music teacher was going to great lengths to tutor me, but I was not progressing very well, so he suggested that if I didn't have time at home to put in the extra practice I so badly needed, perhaps I should stay after school and practice there."

"He even offered to stay and help me. I was just a kid and thought it was nice of him, so I agreed."

Stella paused to see if I knew where this was headed. I put my feet on the coffee table and prepared for a long night.

She went on, "After my last class, I went to the music room, thinking I would practice there, but my tutor suggested we go up to an empty room on the second floor where there would be no interruptions and there was no one to disturb. I thought this was funny, because I knew within fifteen minutes everyone would be gone from the school, but when you are a kid, you think adults know best. We just do what they tell us. There had been a time or two when he made what I know now was inappropriate conversation for him to be having with me, but when you hear adult talk from a teacher, a naïve young girl is sometimes flattered. It seemed like he was just treating me like an adult.

When we went up to the room at the quiet end of the school, I began practicing with my flute. At first he listened closely and made an occasional suggestion. I didn't realize he was just killing time, waiting for the school to empty.

Eventually he asked me to stop and take a break, at which point the conversation became a little uncomfortable. He started asking me about dating and if I was seeing anyone. At first I tried to make conversation, but I quickly figured out where this was going and it was scaring me. I decided to leave."

Stella took a deep breath, got up, made herself another drink and continued, "The next thing I knew, he was kissing me and fondling me and forcing himself up against me. I tried to resist, but he was bigger and stronger than me. I realized then that if I didn't have sex with him willingly, he was going to rape me."

"At that point, my only thought was to escape, so I kneed him in the balls. I wasn't very good at that, and it barely slowed him down, but it provided a split second of hesitation and I broke away and ran out the door. He was two feet behind me and caught me at the railing. He continued roughly fondling me and telling me to come back into the room. I pulled away again, hugging the railing above the walkway, and as he groped for me, he lost his balance. When I saw him falter, I pushed his shoulder and he went over the rail."

I asked what happened next.

Stella said, "It was already evening and there was no one in the school to see it happen, so I grabbed my flute and my purse and left. I didn't tell a soul what happened. When he was found, they couldn't understand what he was doing up on the second floor after school hours, but there was nothing to indicate that this was anything but an accident. There were no witnesses, so we were told that he must have lost his balance and fallen. His neck was broken."

# 23

She took a deep breath like she had just removed something heavy from her shoulders. Looking at me for a moment, she asked, "Do you want me to go on? Or have you heard enough?"

I said, "If there's more, by all means, let it out."

She went on, "About four years later, when I was in a small town in Pennsylvania, working as an appraiser for a Real Estate Company, I went to an office trailer that was being used temporarily as a bank while a new structure was being built. I never frequented that bank, but I needed to cash a check and this was the closest thing to a bank in the immediate area."

"I walked into the middle of a hold-up. As I entered, I was forced to the floor by a man wearing a mask and holding a gun. There were two robbers, one holding a gun on me and the other customers, while the other one collected money from three tellers. When they got all the money, they made me go with them as a hostage. They didn't know the mistake they made grabbing me because since the attempted rape by my teacher, I began carrying a tiny, one shot aerosol can of Mace in my bra."

When we got to their car, they made me get in the back seat and one of the men got in beside me. He was still holding his gun, although it was no longer pointed directly at me. I knew I was in bigger trouble than just a getaway hostage when they took off their masks and let me see their faces. It didn't take a rocket science major to know they would kill me once they were sure they escaped. After we went about five miles on back roads, I wiggled the Mace from my bra and squirted the guy beside me in the face. When he instinctively reacted by reaching for his face, I quickly took the gun from his hand and shot him in the chest."

"Then I stuck the gun to the neck of the driver while the noise was still ringing in my ears, and shouted at him to pull over or I would blow his brains out. When he did, I told him to put the car in park and rest both of his hands on the wheel. He put the car in park, placed his hands on the wheel like I told him and then I shot him in the back of the head."

"I got out of the back seat and used my jacket to wipe my fingerprints from anything I thought I might have touched, although I didn't think I had come in contact with anything but the door handle."

Another deep breath, "I ran about a half mile to a pay phone and called my girlfriend to come get me. I made up a story about an accident so she would come and get me and she was there in short order."

"I never reported it to the police."

Stella continued, "With the temporary trailer being used as a bank, there were no security cameras and no one had a clear view of my face. I was wearing nondescript clothing, nothing that stood out enough to describe me, so the fact was, they couldn't identify me. I knew killing those two assholes wasn't wrong, under the circumstances, and I didn't think the police would arrest me, but I wasn't taking any chances. I had the music teacher's death to which I was afraid of being connected, so I wanted to remain under their radar."

"I knew the bank robbers weren't going to just let me go, so I acted out of fear and necessity, clearly in self-defense. I took a chance and got away with it. Lucky for me, my girlfriend had believed my story and taken me away from there so quickly. She never asked another question about it, and the police were never able to find the girl taken hostage in the bank job."

"By the way, that is where I got this Beretta. It's the one I shot my kidnappers with."

She looked at me like she expected shock, her eyes searching my face for some sign of reaction. What she was seeing was not repulsion but wonderment. I had fallen in love with someone just like me! What were the odds of that? My brain was humming like a swarm of bees at a tulip farm.

It was my turn to talk, so I told her about my escapades, beginning with not making the effort to save Donny, killing Mr. Farmer because he was molesting Wendy, the necessity of killing that sick bastard Kevin, and the drunk in the alley. She agreed that I didn't have choices either.

I told her about the beating in high school that almost killed me and my subsequent smothering of Beaver Shit, I described shooting Sgt. Kellen before he got a whole platoon killed, and told her about Mrs. Starchman and how lucky she was to get a pass because of fate. I explained how I thought my killings were all justifiable and how I didn't know why these things keep happening to me. I said I never thought of myself as a hero, but I supposed in a way, I was. Hero or not, my escapades could never be told, because most of my killings would land me in prison. I was only doing what the law would not do, but a jury would still consider my actions to be murder.

And now, I had Stella, the love of my life, sitting in front of me, telling a chilling, yet similar story.

We were both surprised at the turn of events. She thought it was going to be all over between us when I caught her ready to kill her sister's murderer and I thought I had to keep my past from her for the same reason.

We stayed up talking all night. By morning, we were talked out and exhaustion overtook us when the wildfire of adrenaline finally fizzled out. We eventually went to sleep, with me on the sofa and her on the chair.

It was noon by the time we awoke.

After a Spartan breakfast of instant oatmeal, we reviewed what we had done and if we did it right. I asked Stella if she had ever used the 9mm to shoot anyone besides fat boy in the car and she said she had not. When she killed the two bank robbers with it, she decided to keep it because it felt good to hold and shoot. She knew it was probably an untraceable gun, and the manner in which she acquired it made it a good bet it would not be reported missing. When we examined it from all sides, we thought it might not be safe to keep it any longer. In the three times she had used it, only two were head shots where there probably wouldn't be anything left of the slugs for ballistics to identify, but one was a chest shot, so they might have the gun in the system from that bullet.

We couldn't be sure it wasn't, so we decided to get rid of it. It wouldn't do for the police to track Stella down to question her and then find a gun in her possession that could tie her to a bank robbery. Besides, we had no way of knowing how many other crimes were committed with it, from which a ballistics test could make a connection.

Stella didn't need to be linked to those crimes or any others, so we decided to dump the gun in the Connecticut River, where it would take only a few weeks for the water corrosion to make it unidentifiable.

Fat Boy was mob connected and I had taken his ID, so it would take a while to fingerprint and identify him. The bigger question was, how hard would the cops try to find the killer of a hit man? We agreed that they wouldn't spend a lot of time on it. We feared the mob would look harder for his killer than the cops would, but who could guess? It depended on what his standing was in the mob and whether or not they cared.

He was acting on his own, trying to rob money from the mob too, so they might wonder why he was in Connecticut. There was still the chance that he wasn't going to cheat his bosses, and perhaps they thought he could handle a defenseless girl by himself, but that chance was a slim one. These were all intangibles for which we had no answers. There was no way we could know what the mob was thinking.

We again went carefully over how we did the deed last night to be sure we left nothing at either scene that could lead to us. We left no fingerprints and at that time there was no such thing as DNA, so we both agreed that we did all the right things.

With Stella in the witness protection program, and Fat Boy acting on his own, planning to steal from the mob and kill Stella, we were cautiously confident that the mob wouldn't think twice about her. They might wonder what he was doing so far from home, but we hoped they wouldn't make the connection. As far as we knew, they had no idea where Stella was.

She had contacted Fat Boy, not the other way around, so we thought we were safe from them. We planned on her anonymity remaining intact.

Thankfully, last night had been Friday, so no one expected us at work or anywhere else. We used up most of Saturday sleeping and when we weren't sleeping, we were reassuring ourselves that our tracks were well covered.

Later that afternoon we went for a ride to the Connecticut River, about 15 miles away, and threw the Beretta as far as I could throw it. I knew I would be able to get her another gun. We tossed Fat Boy's .380 in the river too. It would have been foolish to keep either gun. They could be connected to who knows how many crimes. We burned his ID and threw his wallet in the river, but we kept the money.

We went to work on Monday like nothing had happened. There was no news of a body being found over the weekend and we thought the longer it was before they found him, the better.

After work, we compared notes again. Stella was calmer than me. She was feeling some peace, having exacted revenge for Patty's murder. Being of the same mindset as me, she knew in her heart that killing him was the only thing to do.

Stella quietly poked around, getting a feel for anyone asking about her, but she came up empty. As days passed, we became increasingly comfortable that we had come away clean.

In small towns, news spreads like wildfire, so everyone would know within minutes of a body being found, but that news was slow in coming. It was almost three weeks before the word got out that a transient was found dead in a car trunk outside of town. This little town rarely had a murder, so it was the big story for a couple of days. We never heard anything about an investigation, although we knew there was nothing to connect us. At best, they would find out he was a mobster, which should steer any suspicion away from ordinary people. We decided no news was good news.

# 24

It was common knowledge at work that Stella & I were in a relationship, but by now we didn't really care who knew and who didn't. There was no longer any reason to hide it. It's better not to advertise until you're sure of what you have, especially when it's with a co-worker, but we were beyond caring about embarrassment at work if it didn't pan out.

We thought about moving away, but with circumstances being what they were, we didn't want to raise any suspicions, should the investigation of Fat Boy's death involve looking at us. We thought suddenly moving away when a murder is being investigated might raise some eyebrows. Besides, we were young and had plenty of time to shake off the cobwebs of this do-nothing town.

In the end, we decided to make this our home for an indefinite time, despite sharing the same urge to bolt. Cooler heads prevailing and all that.

Stella moved in with me and although my mobile home wasn't anything special, once Stella added a woman's touch to it, our estate became quite nice. It had never been in disrepair, but the truth is, men don't have the knack a woman has for sprucing up a place. A man dusts every six months, whether it needs it or not and thinks he's already doing too much housework.

So here we were.

Life was quiet for a while, considerably quieter than we expected it to be. For a long time, we waited for a knock on the door from the police, with arrest warrants for the murder of Fat Boy, but that knock never came. We had no inside connection to law enforcement, so we never found out what direction the investigation was going, or if there even was one. We tried to be quietly confident there was nothing to worry about concerning Fat Boy's death, but one never knows what could turn up.

The little talk there was indicated that the police couldn't understand what this guy was doing in our little town, carrying no identification, in the trunk of his car with half of his head blown off. We knew his fingerprints would eventually tell them he was a gangster, but that was never confirmed publicly.

There was plenty of speculation floating around town, some being that he was a mobster here to do a hit, or he was someone's secret lover in a relationship gone bad. In reality, most of the people who heard the rumors didn't believe them because you only read about things like this in books or occasionally in the newspaper. Murders never happen in sleepy little towns like Lost River. Not that our sleepy little town didn't have its share of adulterers, drunks and gamblers, because it did, but this was an extremely violent crime.

In most cases, the discovery of a pre-marital or extra-marital dalliance was usually settled with a punch in the nose or a confrontation resulting in a revenge beating. In this town, arguments were never settled with someone's head carved open by a hollow point.

In the meantime, I made a connection with a gun dealer through a guy in another department at work and bought more weapons. I still had my Colt .45 but Stella didn't have a gun anymore and we didn't know when she would have the need to be armed again. Better to have a gun and never need to use it than to be confronted with a life or death situation and not have one. That's how good guys get killed and bad guys stay alive.

After a little haggling and a sizeable amount of money spent, I bought Stella another untraceable 9MM, because she had really liked that Beretta. This was a Sig Sauer semi-automatic with rubber hand grips and a thirteen round magazine. I also bought three extra magazines. I purchased a couple of long guns too. One was a short-barreled 12 gauge Ithaca pump shotgun for Stella and the other was an AR 15 assault rifle for me. I bought a thousand rounds of ammo for each gun. I never wanted to be caught without the means to defend myself. I bought them from a character who brought them from a State where guns don't have to be registered, so although they were brand new, they could never be traced back to me. I was assured they weren't stolen, but there was no way I could be sure of that. I had no intention of being arrested in possession of them anyway, so I put that thought out of my head.

I bought my Colt .45 with no records either, so it wasn't anything new to me to have a gun of questionable origin. That just made them throw-away guns, like Stella's stolen Beretta, when we no longer had a use for them. If we threw them away and they were found, no one would be able to prove they were ever in our possession. When we loaded them, we wore plastic dish-washing gloves, so there were no fingerprints on the shell casings. We weren't paranoid, just cautious.

As far as Fat Boy's killing went, it was finally announced that state and local police finished going through the motions and came up empty. I think they eventually concluded it was a mob hit, which they didn't want any part of, so they simply put it away in a file somewhere. Stella and I put it to rest too.

# 25

Then one day, despite having only lived in Lost River for a little over a year, I received a summons ordering me to report for jury duty in Superior Court in Hartford. I had never served on a jury before and it wasn't my desire to serve now, but I thought no harm would be done because any dummy can get out of jury duty if he has half a brain. Someone famous once said they wouldn't want to have their future decided by 12 people who were too stupid to get out of jury duty. I was of the same mind.

I nevertheless decided that it might be a kick seeing some asshole get his just reward through the legal system for a change, instead of having justice handed out by someone like me. So far, my experience had been that true justice came only at my hand.

Of course, I only recently learned that Stella had done her fair share of handing out that kind of justice too. There were few choices for either of us, because you don't know how impotent law enforcement is until you need it to work for you and it's not there. If the law had been able to find Fat Boy, Stella wouldn't have had to go into the program and she wouldn't have had to blow his brains out. Funny that the law couldn't find him, but she could. It seems like the FBI is good at coming by and taking statements after the fact, but that doesn't help the dead victim. If more people stood up for their rights and were allowed to protect their lives and property, there would be a lot less crime.

When it became my day to report to the court, I showed up at the prescribed time and spent the first two hours bored to death, with nothing to do before my number was called. When it was, I went to a courtroom with well over a hundred other people, where the judge and the lawyers could sort out who was and wasn't fit to be a juror. Nobody spoke with anyone, but you could see in everyone's eyes that we had a common goal. We all wanted to get out of this as fast as possible.

I had never been called for this before, so I didn't know what to expect other than what I might have seen on television. I don't think anyone expected it to be like television and we were correct in that assumption, because it wasn't. I sat and watched twelve people called to the jury box, along with three alternates. Evidently they swear in alternates to replace any juror who gets sick or must leave for some reason before the trial is completed.

Once the twelve were seated, the judge went into a harangue about how everyone was sworn to secrecy. He described the penalties for corresponding with a newspaper or television reporter and all of that drivel. A mistrial would be declared if that happened and they would have to start over. He stressed that anyone involved with the case wasn't allowed to discuss the trial, even with each other. He also ruled that no juror is allowed to conduct any form of investigation on their own, is not allowed to go to any crime scene or read about it or watch television reports about the alleged crime or the trial. He said the votes of the jurors are supposed to be derived strictly from what the attorneys on both sides are able to convince them to believe. I only half listened because I was bored and just wanted out as badly as the rest of my fellow prospective jurors.

Then something happened that captured my attention. The judge told us this was a criminal case against a man named Roland Masters, seated at a table in front of us, with his attorneys. He was charged with numerous counts of molesting a girl under the age of twelve. He was a janitor at West Elementary School, where the child attended. He was charged with, among other things, fondling her, making her touch him and having oral copulation with her on more than one occasion. The charges were labeled "Criminal Assault on a Minor." After numerous alleged assaults by him, the girl finally told her mother about them, and her mother called the authorities. Roland Masters looked to be in his late forties, a somewhat overweight white guy with long shiny black hair streaked in front with gray. His hair was pulled back into a ponytail and tied with a green rubber band.

He had myriad of ugly tattoos which I would have covered if I was on trial for something this disgusting. They made him look like a convict. One could assume he wasn't particularly smart to openly display them. You could likewise question his attorney's level of competence for not advising him to keep them covered.

Roland was not a handsome man, carrying unsightly scars on the left side of his face and neck. His nose must have been broken a few times because it made a right turn which looked very unnatural. The permanent sneer on his face wasn't helping his appearance either. One had to wonder what kind of school department would hire someone like this to work around young children. His appearance spoke volumes.

In my mind I already knew he was guilty.

They began the questioning phase and slow weeding out of prospective jurors, replacing them with people still sitting in the jury pool. It looked like it was going to be a long selection process. By now, I was looking forward to seeing this asshole taken away in shackles, so I was happy when they called me to the jury box after about three hours into the selection procedure.

I was welcomed by the judge, who made sure I understood the complexities of being a juror and the seriousness of any decision I would make about the defendant's innocence or guilt. I had been sitting there for hours, listening to him give the same speech to all of the prospective jurors, so I was primed and easily assured him that I fully understood what was at stake. He asked me a lot of personal questions that almost had me wondering who the fuck was on trial here. I gave mostly neutral answers about my opinions and he seemed satisfied with that.

I wondered what his reaction would be if I recounted my experiences in killing people like Roland Masters.

Both attorneys questioned me and continued questioning the other prospective jurors, slowly weeding out the weirdos, the overly timid, the loudmouths and the wise guys. Oddly, they also weeded out engineers and any lawyers who had been summoned. They dismissed policemen and those who had a relative or close friend in law enforcement. Everyone who had personal experience with a case of child molestation, child endangerment or domestic violence was quickly dismissed as well. They also released people who appeared to have too much intelligence.

Evidently they wanted a jury of sheep, so to stay on the jury and see this thing through, I had to pretend to be someone other than myself. The attorneys didn't want jurors who were smarter than them.

Eventually, after two days of questioning me and countless other prospects, I made the final cut and became Juror Number 289 in a seated jury of six men and six women. Two of the women were from somewhere in the Orient and there was one black guy. The rest of us were white.

Then an unexpected thing happened. The day after we were seated on the jury, we were lounging in the jury room, waiting to be called into the courtroom and I was snacking on a gooey energy bar. When I was finished with it, I looked for a trash can to get rid of the wrapper and found one next to an unattended bailiff's station, so I walked over to toss in the wrapper. To my dismay, I missed the rectangular basket by a foot and the gooey wrapper landed on the floor. When I bent down to pick it up and place it more carefully in the basket, I saw an official looking piece of paper on top of the trash already in the basket. The paper looked like it said something about "Minute" and "Suppression" on it. Being the curious man I am, I palmed the paper and stuck it in my pocket.

When we were brought into the courtroom and the Judge came in, he read the thirteen counts against the shitbag sitting in front of us. Then the lawyers did their best to explain what the charges meant, as if we were too stupid to understand English.

The prosecuting attorney told us he was going to prove how badly this little girl had been traumatized when on numerous occasions the defendant touched her inside her panties while kissing her, and putting his tongue in her mouth. Then, as these occasions became more frequent, he had coaxed her to touch him, while telling her it was alright because she was almost an adult now and this is what big girls did. As time went by, he became more aggressive and daring, but did not penetrate her vagina. The prosecutor then claimed that on several occasions, the defendant persuaded her to perform oral sex on him.

After the fourth time he did this, when during the act he climaxed, she told her mother what had happened.

The defense attorney tried to make light of the charges, saying that little girls have vivid imaginations and how they are exposed to sexual situations in books, in the movies and on television and how sometimes they make up stories just to garner attention. Then he told us that the way the law is written, the lines are quite blurry for the term "Oral Copulation," and that the accusation isn't always as bad as the term makes it sound. His contention was that even putting one's tongue in an alleged victim's mouth is considered oral copulation under the current state statutes. I never knew that.

He explained how he was going to prove that this little girl was a troublemaker in school and he went on and on with other accusatory bullshit that I pretty much tuned out. I was concentrating on looking closely at the scumbag on trial and observing his facial expressions and body language. Having had my share of experiences with child molesters long before coming here, I knew Roland Masters was guilty as sure as Cain killed Abel.

That afternoon, after being excused for the day, I took out the paper I had removed from the trash and read it. It was called a "Minute Order," which was a list of evidence that the judge had ruled inadmissible and was ordering suppressed from the jury. It got my attention because it didn't make sense that there would be proof of the defendant's guilt or innocence being withheld from the jury for any reason.

After reading it, the long and short of it was, the judge has the power to suppress any and all evidence he chooses. In this case, he was not allowing any testimony or reference to two previous accusations of child annoyance made against the defendant, nor would he allow into evidence child pornography that was found in Master's home. It did not indicate why this damning behavior wasn't going to be presented as evidence of Roland's lack of character and previous unlawful actions. I guessed I really didn't understand the judicial system. It was just further proof to me that this guy was the shitbag I thought he was. Yet the law says his character can't be tainted by evidence of past behavior? How absurd can that be? Things he did in the past can't be presented for fear it might sway the favor of the jury? That was the most ridiculous thing I ever heard.

Before the trial began, we were on the receiving end of a long lecture from the judge about how our personal opinion of the defendant, the attorneys, or our opinions of the laws and what we think they should be, were all inconsequential. We were there to decide the guilt or innocence of the defendant based entirely on what was proven to us by the opposing attorneys. The judge made it clear that he is the power in the courtroom, and will instruct us on what is and isn't allowed. What he was saying was, in our hearts we may be sure this bastard is guilty, but if the prosecution has not given us that last thread of evidence proving guilt without a reasonable doubt, the law requires a "Not Guilty" verdict.

I never heard such bullshit in my life. Most of the judge's lecture had no effect on me whatsoever, other than proving that the laws are made for the lawbreakers. No one gives a damn about the victims. Of course, I had information the other jurors didn't have, but I couldn't reveal what I knew. To do that would result in a mistrial. I knew in my soul that this guy was guilty and unless the defense attorney could prove without a reasonable doubt that he was innocent, I wanted to see him hung by his balls.

The trial finally began. The reality of the trial was in itself an exercise in useless bantering between the attorneys, as to who was speaking out of line and who wasn't, with many objections from both of the lead attorneys over the tactics of the other. At first, it was handled quite fairly by the judge. The way the judge presided over the case with fairness and respect toward the defendant and all of the attorneys present, it would appear that he must be a fair man. I had seen the suppressed evidence, so I knew better.

The prosecution called the girl's mother and asked her to recall her daughter's confession about what went on and to tell about her little girl's frame of mind, mental anguish and hysteria in telling her mother the grim details. She was asked about her own reaction upon hearing this from her daughter and much about the handling of the accusations by police. Of course, the defense attorney objected every two minutes, saying that the mother's reaction was irrelevant. As I expected, the judge sustained most of his objections.

The prosecution brought the arresting officers, the lady officer who had taken the little girl's statement, a psychologist who had counseled the girl and a pair of women teachers who taught her in elementary school. Eventually they brought the little girl to the witness stand.

The prosecuting attorney walked the girl through the whole procession of testifying, coaxing her to tell her story, which she did with amazing clarity for a girl of her age in a room full of strangers. She broke down a few times, especially when she got to the part about the blowjobs this motherless fuck had forced her to do. I thought it was obvious that she couldn't have been making up such an elaborate story.

When the prosecutor was done with her, the Judge called a recess for the day.

The next morning, the defense attorney had his turn and began by quietly asking the girl if she ever watched prime time television. She replied that she did. He asked her about a half dozen TV shows which I personally agreed were far too sexually explicit for young people to be watching. Many of them she had seen while some she had not. Then he asked her about "R" rated movies, named a few, and asked if she had ever seen them. There were a few that she answered with a yes. Then he asked her if, when they were talking about sexual situations on TV or in a movie, or when there was nudity, was she aware of what they were talking about and did she know what was happening. She said for the most part, she did. When asked how she knew so much about sex, she said her mother had explained a lot about reproduction to her and all of the girls at school talked about it quite often.

When asked if she knew what oral sex was before she engaged in it, a roar came from the prosecuting attorney strongly objecting to the direction the defense attorney was headed. The judge overruled his objection even though it was clear that this question about her knowledge of oral sex was a trick to make it look like she was confessing to participating in oral sex with someone other than the defendant. It was an obvious ploy to make the jury think this wasn't new to her.

The defense attorney asked the little girl the most private and intimate questions about her experiences with boys, with girls, anyone she may have seen in sexual situations, petting and to what extent her experiences were. He asked if any petting she may have experienced was done over or underneath clothing, what body parts were touched and how often she had done this. Before long the little girl was in tears and admitted to having a few of these petting sessions with boys from school.

I hoped the jurors would look back at their own lives as curious children and recall the times they experimented with other kids. Those experiences are quite normal when you are young. We all did it, so they shouldn't let her confession cloud their judgment of her.

Then they brought in character witnesses for the defendant. It was a sight to behold. I wouldn't have wanted to have these yahoos vouching for my character. They all had long greasy hair, wore tattoos, some of which bordered on obscene and they looked like degenerates on parole. They would probably all be back in prison soon.

After eight days of grueling testimony from character witnesses, friends and the little girl herself, and hearing each attorney's closing arguments, the case was finally turned over to the jurors, with no testimony from the defendant. Before we were sent to the deliberation room, the judge gave us another long lecture reminding us that the defendant had the right to have his case decided by what the law says, not what anyone's personal feelings were and that it was our duty to review what the attorneys said and the evidence they presented. We were expected to make a fair decision based solely on that.

# 26

No one on the jury had any experience being a foreman, so in the end we elected the black guy for no reason in particular. He seemed somewhat versed in the procedures for us to follow in our deliberations and eventual verdict. My mind was already made up and if the punishment was going to involve hanging, I wanted to go buy the rope. After much talk about what we should do and where we should start, we finally agreed to first take a secret ballot vote just to see where we stood. I thought we would be out of there in five minutes. It was a no-brainer.

It turned out there were three votes for a guilty verdict and nine for acquittal. I was dumbfounded. In my mind this shitbag was as guilty as hell. It was unimaginable that there could be people anywhere who thought he was innocent, let alone nine out of twelve.

After that stunning vote, we took turns discussing the evidence, what we thought about the defendant, what we thought of the little girl's testimony, the lawyers and even the judge. I expected the women to be sympathetic toward the victim, but it turned out they were bleeding hearts, unable to bring themselves to vote for a guilty verdict because they felt there was an outside chance the defendant was innocent. Most of them admitted they thought he was probably guilty, but were afraid of sending an innocent man to prison.

My argument was, suppose he is guilty and gets away with what he has done? Were we ready to turn him loose to molest another little girl, or a half dozen little girls?

When it was my turn to speak, I pointed out how I interpreted his looks and demeanor to indicate a total lack of character along with the friends he brought to court to vouch for him. I spoke of my doubts that a little girl would make this kind of accusation unless there was some truth to it and questioned how she could know the things she knew if she hadn't experienced it. I was on the receiving end of arguments that it's not Christian to judge a man by how he looks, that tattoos are acceptable today and how his friends were just poor people who looked the way they looked from being poor. I argued that for poor people, they all had money for tattoos and piercings but that argument went nowhere.

I tried a different tact, asking the bleeding hearts among us how they would feel if they let this scumbag go and he molested their daughter or granddaughter. Despite being as calm as I could be in my arguments, I was met with ridicule and found my credibility being discounted and myself being regarded as some kind of radical. By this time, I was speechless.

The attorney for the defense had done a convincing job of pointing out all of the things about sex that a child doesn't need to experience to know about today, because of television, movies and the general permissiveness of our decaying present day society. I didn't win there either.

I lost all of my arguments and by the time we took our third vote, I was the lone dissenter. After relentless browbeating from the other jurors, I finally gave in. It was obvious I was not going to change eleven minds, so I surrendered and agreed go along with the rest of the jurors. The bleeding hearts congratulated themselves on turning around the lone dissenter, and this low-life was found not guilty on all counts.

The defendant and his attorneys were all smiles, shaking hands and patting each other on the back, and the jurors were proud to have done the right thing in letting this poor maligned man go free. But I knew better.

I was not done with Roland Masters.

# 27

Stella was livid when I told her the verdict and I couldn't blame her. Considering the things we both experienced with sex offenders and perverts, and what we did in the past when in situations with predators, we thought we were justified in our outrage. This trial brought back vivid memories which became the topic of the day almost every day. We recounted our thoughts about how wrong it is that so many despicable people commit terrible acts upon innocent children. Worse is that so many get away with it because of simple-minded fools who feel sorrier for the perpetrators than they do for the innocent victims.

After hours of bitching, I offhandedly suggested we should kill this bastard ourselves. That opened another avenue of discussion about all the "what ifs." What if we decided to take a hand in meting out a little justice of our own. There was nothing we could do for the poor little girl whose innocence was taken away by this low life son-of-a-bitch, but we sure could prevent him from harming any more children. It was not our intent to become avenging angels but surely, someone has to stop the monsters. If the law enforcement agencies hands were tied and the judicial system in the state couldn't or wouldn't do it, maybe we should.

We didn't have much to go on besides his name and, of course, knowing what he looked like. Stella had seen his picture in the newspaper many times, so she would recognize him too. We decided the first thing to do would be to determine where he lived and what his routines were. Mind you, we still didn't have a plan. We simply thought we could begin by observing his everyday life and perhaps something would give us an idea about how to get to him undetected. If we were going to tail him to find out his routine, Stella was going to have to do most of the legwork. He had seen me every day of the trial and I was afraid he would easily recognize me.

Masters wasn't hard to find. He lived not too far from the school where he still worked, in a single family home, surrounded by a neighborhood that was very run down. After watching him for a few weeks, mostly after our work shifts were over, we found that Roland liked to frequent a seedy little bar called "The Getaway" in the next town. It was about fifteen miles away. We thought with all the publicity in our town about his case, perhaps he hoped he wouldn't be easily recognized in another venue. Small towns gossip and although this case didn't warrant much air time on television and almost no front page headlines, there must surely be neighbors or irate parents to harass him or perhaps worse. We thought that might be why he chose to spend his evenings at The Getaway.

Often, small town people like to keep to themselves and stay in their cocoons, so chances of being singled out and harassed would be greatly diminished if he did his drinking at a bar fifteen miles away. In any case, it's easy to tell the difference between country folks and city folks. The country folks don't feel like they belong anywhere but at home, so people from Lost River were not likely to run into him at The Getaway. It would be a different story if he lived in a city because city folks will go anywhere.

After watching Roland patronize The Getaway almost every night, we decided Stella should probably go in there by herself for a cocktail, just to observe. We watched from my car at the far end of the parking lot away from the dim lights of the bar, where we would most likely not be seen. We wanted to get a feel for how long he stayed and what we could learn about his habits. It wouldn't do to whack him, if that was actually what we were going to do, and find out afterward that he had someone watching his back.

After spending a week sitting in my car with nothing exciting happening, we knew it was time to go with our original idea and send Stella in. She fully expected him to hit on her before she was there very long. With her stunning looks, I thought she was right. Most of the women we watched go into The Getaway in a week of surveillance were a mighty homely bunch. Of course, the term homely is relative to how much you've had to drink. When we watched them, I was sober, and I didn't think I could consume enough alcohol to make any of those dogs look good.

The night Stella went in for a cocktail, she purposely dressed down so she wouldn't stand out too much among the ladies we had observed frequenting the bar. I jokingly supposed they named it "The Getaway" because it was a good place for the lady patrons to get away from the dog catcher.

The first time Stella went into The Getaway, we were nervous because there was no way for her to contact me if something unexpected happened. It didn't turn out as bad as we feared, because strangely enough, except for an occasional guy asking if she needed another drink, she wasn't really hit on. She just nursed the margarita she had for about an hour. Roland never looked at her.

When she came out and we drove away, we talked at length about what she should do to eventually lure him away from the bar, so I could do my part in whatever we were going to do. We were still in the planning stage and didn't know how we were going to dish out his comeuppance. By this time I made up my mind I was going to kill him if I had the chance and Stella knew it.

My experiences told me that using a gun was the quickest, most effective way to kill someone, but we were wary of going that route for fear of a gunshot being too easily heard. Unlike in the movies, we had no silencers for our guns. If people were close enough to hear shots, help might arrive before we could get away from the scene. We hadn't decided yet where the "scene" would be or if this was even going to work. So far we were mostly talk, but in considering the methods we could use to kill him besides using a gun, all of the alternatives sounded pretty uninviting.

I didn't entertain strangulation for a couple of reasons. First, that would mean a struggle and there were no guarantees of me coming out on top in that kind of confrontation. I couldn't imagine knifing him either. I guess I would rather have no physical challenge, so that took us back to a shooting. I didn't have any idea where I could get a silencer for my .45 and the homemade silencers we had heard of and read about seemed a bit foolhardy. I couldn't envision Masters standing still while I stuck a potato on the end of my gun so I could shoot him quietly.

Despite throwing Kevin into the cement, suffocating Beaver Shit while he was unconscious, and the drunk in the alley, I didn't relish the idea of killing anyone with my bare hands. In Beaver Shit's case, I had kicked him unconscious and then simply shut off his air supply while he was out, so I didn't categorize that as a strangulation killing. I couldn't entertain killing someone in a bare handed knuckle-buster because it could be chancy and too easy to lose. We needed to be more creative.

Despite weeks of frequenting The Getaway every few nights, Stella had not been able to attract the attention of our child molester, but we were not going to give up just yet. We thought that with his desires being what they were, he evidently wasn't interested in an encounter with an adult. We weren't going to use a child for bait, so we stubbornly continued with the original plan, such as it was. We were sure that sooner or later we would lure him out of the bar. What we did after we isolated him was yet to be decided.

# 28

We thought perhaps we were leaving the bar too soon, so one night we decided Stella should not leave until after Roland left, thinking perhaps he would wait in the parking lot and strike up a conversation with her. Then she could subtly show some interest. We were grasping at straws because he wasn't cooperating and as long as he didn't, our plan remained a "no plan." After a week of doing this, it appeared Roland was not going to develop an interest in Stella anytime soon, so we mulled over what could be the best thing to do in revising our non-plan.

One Thursday night, after Roland left the Getaway, Stella came out fifteen minutes later and got in the car. We slowly left the parking lot and drove down the dark, deserted road that led back to our home, once again disappointed that Roland was showing no interest.

About two miles into the ride home, we saw a car on the shoulder with its hood up. Surprisingly, it was Roland's Impala and he was standing in the road waving his arms for us to stop. Our immediate thought was that he was on to us and this was a trap. The thought quickly vanished, however, because I knew he had never seen us together and probably wouldn't know what kind of car to look for if he had.

I rolled to a stop behind his car, under a painfully dim streetlight, and he came over to my window. I rolled it down like anyone would, so he could tell me why he was stopping us.

He looked in the car and to our surprise, showed no sign that he recognized me, but saw Stella and said, "Hey, I know you! I see you almost every night at The Getaway!"

Stella smiled and answered, "Yes, I've been going there quite often lately."

He smiled back and now addressed me, still unaware of my identity, "Something has happened to my car. I don't know what, but it just conked out. Do you know anything about cars?"

I figured he was so upset about his car that he had not yet realized I was one of his jurors. I guessed when he was on trial for his perverted activities he didn't look at the jury very much. Mostly, he watched his attorneys and when he wasn't watching them or whoever was on the witness stand, he was looking at the floor.

I replied, "I have a little knowledge of cars, but I'm no mechanic. What do you think happened?"

Roland said, "I was just driving along and the headlights got dim and then it stalled."

I suggested that maybe his battery was dead. I didn't know what I could do, but said I would look at it.

Stella and I got out of my car and walked over to his Chevy, which was warm from driving even though it had only been driven a few miles. As nervous as I was, I kept my voice calm and asked, "Has it been starting OK?" He said it had been but now when you turn the key, nothing happens, so I suggested he might just have a loose battery cable.

By now, Stella and I were both trying to figure out what was going on. The last thing we wanted to do was to get warm and fuzzy with this asshole. If we even had a plan, it wouldn't have included anything like this. Then it got better.

We looked at the battery terminals, neither of which seemed to be in very good condition. He wiggled them around a little and tried the key and still had nothing. He either didn't have money for a tow truck or thought we would give him a ride if needed. He acted like he really wanted to get home. The thought of getting this close to

Roland was chilling enough without thinking about having him inside my car, so I didn't discourage him from trying to get his Impala started.

He was not having any luck and then said, "I have a friend who had this problem once and all he did was tap on the battery terminals with a hammer and his car started afterward. I think I have one in the trunk. It's worth a try, huh?"

At that moment, my internal red lights began to flash. I worried that he was going to the trunk to grab a gun or something, but when he came around from the rear of the car, all he held was a hickory-handled Ball Peen hammer which looked like it weighed about three pounds. It appeared very well used.

He asked Stella if she would mind turning the key while he tapped the terminals. After a quick, questioning look at me, she slid behind the wheel. Roland tapped both terminals a couple of times while she turned the key. Still nothing happened.

He suggested that in the dark, if there was any kind of spark from a loose connection, it should be much more visible than it would be in the daytime, so he asked if I would tap the terminals while he tried to get a better look at the connections.

Then this fucking dipshit handed me the hammer. I gave Stella a look that said, "It can't be this easy, can it?"

He said, "OK, young lady, turn the key!" Then he bent over to get a better look at the underside of the battery terminals. I stood there holding the hammer like I never saw one before.

Roland looked at me and said, "Go ahead! Tap it! You can't hurt anything!"

I guess that was the urging I needed because without another moment of thought or hesitation, when he leaned in front of me again, I swung the freaking hammer like Thor on a tempestuous night, and landed a blow just over his right ear. He grunted and swayed a little, but did not fall, so I swung the hammer harder and hit him again in the same place.

This time Masters dropped like a heart-shot buck. He never uttered another sound, he just fell. When he did, the front of his head bounced on the grill, propelling him backwards and the back of his head whacked on the asphalt. It sounded like someone pounding a steak with a large wooden tenderizer.

Stella jumped out of the car and yelled, "What the fuck just happened?"

I shakily answered, "I'm not sure, but we better get the hell out of here before someone drives by and sees this!"

Looking quickly in both directions, I saw nothing but darkness, so I quickly checked him for a pulse. There was one, but it was weak, so I swung the hammer one more time, hitting him directly on the temple. I could hear his skull crunch as the hammer found its mark.

I checked again for a pulse. Finding none, I took his keys out of the ignition, stuck them in my pocket and using my handkerchief, I quickly wiped the door handle, steering wheel and all around the shift lever and ignition. Stella said she had not touched anything but the key, but we needed to be sure. After the hurried wipe-down, we jumped into my car and got gone from there.

We drove directly home, pausing momentarily on the rusted metal-framed bridge separating the townships where I threw his keys and the guilty hammer into the creek below. When we arrived home, we went directly inside, knowing we had to have our story straight if and when the police came. We were each other's alibi, but Stella had likely been seen at The Getaway earlier that evening. Whether or not anyone paid attention to when she left or in what direction she went was anyone's guess.

Our biggest fear was the authorities would start connecting the dots and put together me having been a juror in Masters' child molestation trial, the one who had unsuccessfully lobbied for his conviction. Add to that, Stella & I living together, and I didn't think the police were that dumb. Sooner or later, they were going to get suspicious and start adding up the coincidences.

We decided we should get out of town for a couple of days to strengthen our alibi for each other.

We grabbed clothes from our dressers, hopped in my car and drove in the opposite direction by a roundabout route, to a campground over sixty miles away, where you paid with cash in an envelope for a campsite. No one would know what time we arrived other than what we wrote on the registration form. There was a round, slotted container nailed to a stump for just that purpose.

It was approaching two in the morning when we pulled into the campground and since it was a week night, there were no other campers there to see us come in. I wrote nine o'clock as our arrival time on the form.

We drove into the empty campground, picked out a spot away from the road, backed into the parking slot so we could get out of there quickly if necessary and called it a night.

Sleep was elusive and what little rest we did get was not very comforting in the car. We lightly dozed, but woke up often, looking forward to sunrise. It came eventually and we were aroused by the first streaks of light, wishing we had some coffee, knowing we didn't. We were determined to stay there at least until noon, but we took a short jaunt to a gas station pay phone about a mile away, to call work. We left messages with our department heads that we were sick. We had forgotten about having to work the next day, so it was fortunate there was a pay-phone that close by. We also picked up coffee and doughnuts at the gas station to help clear the lingering fog.

At about ten o'clock, a park ranger came through and collected our six dollars from the can on the stump. He drove through the campground, waved as he went by, and left without a word. I was glad someone saw us and had a record of us being there, many miles from the murder site.

We stayed another night and returned home the next day by the same route we came, closely obeying the speed limits and coming to full stops wherever it was required.

This was Saturday, which meant no work tomorrow, so we hunkered down to wait for the police to come. They never did.

We watched with great interest as the story was reported on television that a man recently acquitted in a trial over morals charges was found dead on a lonely road, apparently bludgeoned to death with a blunt object. The newscast said he had been seen earlier that evening at a bar called The Getaway, about twenty miles from where he lived.

Rumor had it the police were looking at relatives of the child he was connected with in the recent molestation case. They were obviously looking into a revenge angle.

Weeks went by and we were living a somewhat normal life, for people in fear of being arrested at any time and charged with murder. We were always sure of where we kept the receipt from the campground and exactly what our story was. As far as anyone would know, we were just a pair of horny young people who simply wanted to get away and spend a night fucking in the woods.

We never had to use the receipt or our story.

Within a month following Roland's death, seven more girls, mostly in their early teens, reported to police that they had been harassed, felt up, licked and who knows what else, by Roland. Many of his accusers said these things happened when they were preteens. That removed any doubt that Roland Masters was guilty of the crimes for which he had been acquitted.

After that, the police more or less shelved any further pursuit of Roland's killer, unofficially deciding perhaps justice had been served. Nobody cared that someone had killed a child molester.

# 29

Stella and I wanted to get away from this town and the troubles that went down here, but we thought if we left suddenly, it might trigger some ambitious lawman with nothing else to do, to notice our sudden departure, and wonder if there was a reason for it. Small town police are very aware of people coming and going.

I thought we were lucky to have done the deeds we did here without raising any eyebrows. All it would have taken for us to be caught was if someone had come along, in the wrong place at the wrong time and seen us kill Fat Boy or Roland Masters. That didn't happen, but luck like that wasn't going to last forever. Although we had reservations about leaving the area so quickly after the recent crimes reported, we agreed the sooner we left this small town, the sooner we would just be a fading memory.

There were pros and cons to living in Lost River. The good part was, as long as something else came along to lure the authorities off the scent, their manpower was such that they would quickly drop old news for new news. The bad thing was, big things like murder don't happen often here, so we were constantly afraid one day a competent investigator could come along and make a connection or two. We decided it would be better to be gone, so we moved forward on a plan to leave.

I had developed a case of wanderlust and evidently it was rubbing off on Stella, so we got serious about a new life somewhere else. It increasingly became a topic of discussion when enjoying a drink or two. We decided to cash out, buy a van and travel for a while, under the radar. Hopefully our trail would cool off for whoever might be trying to find us, whether it was the mob or the law. We both loved camping, so we thought about trying that for a while.

We stuck it out another six months, staying through the coldest of the winter months and then put the mobile home up for sale. It took almost four months to sell. While we were planning, we found a good buy on a barely used Ford travel van with very low miles. It was a white, long wheel base model, so it had room to spare inside. There was a sofa in the very back that folded down into a bed, but it wasn't nearly big enough for me to stretch out on, so using that for sleeping was out of the question. I preferred a tent anyway.

I removed the sofa and the back seat captain's chairs and installed a custom, folding bed to use when it rained or otherwise wouldn't be prudent to sleep in a tent or under the stars.

We talked excitedly about dropping out and going on the road, maybe for quite a while. Stella was looking forward to it as much if not more than me. She wanted to put all of her sordid history behind her and begin a new life with me, away from here, with no cares and no one chasing her. If Fat Boy's buddies ever figured out what happened to him, we would be long gone and her trail would be cold. Hopefully they would call off their search for her and we could live in peace.

Dropping out required Stella to break the one tie she had with the Witness Protection System, but she wanted to break the connection there anyway. She lived in fear of a slip-up or a glitch somewhere within the Program that would reveal how she could be found. It wouldn't do for the mob to find that glitch and locate her because of some clerk's mistake. Chances were her Program connection would be just as happy when they couldn't find her. It would be one less responsibility for them and one less headache on someone's caseload.

We sold the mobile home for almost twice what I paid for it, and sold our possessions and both cars. With what we got for all of that, the money I had saved from my Army days and what Stella and I saved while working at the aircraft plant, we were starting our new life with no financial worries. Even with the expenditure of the van and all of the extras we customized it with, we were beginning a new, nomadic life with a little over sixty-six thousand dollars. We kept ten thousand in cash and put the rest in two different well-known national banks. With bank checks to use against the balance, which could be used as cash or to access cash from anywhere, money wouldn't be a problem. Both banks issued credit cards with high credit lines, which could come in handy if we needed to use them.

We arranged payment for bills, such as van registration and insurance and credit cards, directly from our savings accounts. For the purpose of residency requirements needed for registration, licenses and insurance, we used the address of a mail house where we obtained a PO Box. We thought it would be easy to simply drop out of society and disappear, but there's more to it than just leaving town. There were still some things for which we needed to have an address, even if it was just a building with a mail box in our names. As long as there was a physical address with a street number, everyone was happy and there were no questions asked.

We made lists of things we had to do and undo and preparations to be made, hoping we could think of everything. We felt like we were finally going to be free. With no financial obligations and enough cash to last for at least a couple of years of frugal living we were pretty confident about the future.

The van was a year old and sported fewer than three thousand miles, so it was like new. After taking out the sofa and putting in the folding bed, it still had enough room to put in a tiny combination gas and electric fridge. We installed a porta-potty behind the driver's seat, and enclosed it with a u-shaped rod and a shower curtain for privacy. I bought a lightweight fiberglass roof top carryall from a camper specialty store, which I mounted on the luggage rails on the roof. It provided ample room to store all the clothes we wanted to bring. It didn't look very big, but the appearance was deceiving. It held much more than we thought, yet it was quite aerodynamic.

We bought a small propane fueled two-burner camp cook stove and two propane lanterns which could be used for heat as well as light. In my experience, they can heat up a tent as well as a propane heater and give off all the light you could want without sucking out oxygen. This eliminated the need for a separate heater unit, unless temperatures were frigid. We planned to be in a warm climate by the time winter arrived, so that shouldn't be a factor.

We hung two fold-up, bagged chairs to a bracket I installed on the inside of the rear doors, because sitting on the ground around a campfire gets old quickly. I bought two five-speed bicycles, and installed a hitch and a bike rack on the back of the van to carry them. We also found a fourteen by sixteen foot, two room, peak-roofed tent at an Army/Navy Survival Store which would serve extremely well for sleeping and living outdoors. The tubing for the tent was a light-weight, polymer material that would stay flexible without breaking, even in the cold.

We purchased a queen-sized air mattress with a battery operated pump that, flattened and folded, fit splendidly under the bed in the van, along with a couple of sleeping bags and blankets. When inflated, the air mattress stood over two feet off the floor so it wouldn't feel like we were sleeping on the ground. We also picked up a couple of bedrolls and ground sheets, in case we decided to go off hiking somewhere and were planning to sleep under the stars.

We left ourselves options for whatever we wanted to do at any particular time. One never knows.

Under the driver's seat, I stored a more than adequate first aid kit and stocked plenty of insect repellent and water purification tablets to ensure safety if we needed to drink stream water. We purchased waterproof ponchos, waterproof hiking boots, thick military style socks for padding and a tin of foot powder. I added a 100ft. coil of rope and a dozen safety flares to our supplies. We put in a stock of extra flashlight batteries and five butane lighters. We had "strike-anywhere" matches, but we didn't want to be stuck without fire if the matches accidentally became wet. We brought a four-cup, hot and cold thermos with an insulated pouch which could attach to a pistol belt or backpack. This would be good for carrying hot soup or coffee when we were going to be away from a heat source.

We planned to do most of our sleeping in the tent and almost all of our time outdoors, but would need the van for traveling and to sleep in when it was rainy or cold. Our handguns fit nicely in the storage slots on the door panels and we stored the long guns behind our seats for easy access. Lessons we learned from past experiences taught us that preparation and planning was the key to staying alive. We were obsessed with expecting the unexpected and being ready for it.

Beneath the floor of the van, I added a flat, five-gallon, propane operated hot water heater and a fifteen-gallon fresh water holder, with a twelve volt pump. The water heater was designed to only heat when you needed hot water, rather than having one that was always on. We bought a self-standing outdoor shower curtain, which opened easily to provide privacy when showering. It nicely folded into a small bag when not in use for easy storage.

In a sporting goods store I found a flat, black twenty-four inch square rubber that was mostly designed to be a sports marker or base of some kind. We could use this as a platform to stand on when showering outdoors. Less than a half-inch thick, it also took up a minimum of storage space, and would help with foot hygiene in the wild.

It was an interesting challenge to cover all the bases for practicality and ease of access while traveling long-term. Just when we thought we had everything we needed, we thought of something else. We went to a camping and outdoor living specialty store in Hartford and bought several maps showing the thousands of places around the country where you could go off by yourself without using campgrounds, to avoid paying for camping. Campground fees don't seem like much for a night or two, but for everyday living, they can eat your finances up quickly. Besides, we wanted to get away from people in general.

It was my experience that campground people are sometimes too interested in socializing and other people's business. We didn't want to become involved with anyone for a while. We were tired of this life and looking over our shoulders all the time. We wanted solitude, a respite from town living and most of all, a different take on life from the one we were leaving.

We talked at length about the changes in our lives, and although we didn't spend much time talking about long-term relationships, we both agreed that we were totally committed to each other. We were with the partner we wanted to spend forever with and there was no reason to think anyone or anything could change that. We were old enough to know we had a great thing and knew how lucky we were to be in the place we were. We spent many evenings professing our love for each other and were thankful to have found each other when neither of us thought we ever would. Marriage would happen eventually, but at this time, it really wasn't important. We were just going to enjoy each other and freedom.

Before we packed up and left, we had a discussion about another important topic. The elephant in the room was the talk we needed to have about putting an end to the killings. Life was going to be different from now on, and we needed to close that chapter. We were of the same mind that we had only killed people who needed killing, or in self-defense. But we knew that if the killings continued, it would only be a matter of time before someone stumbled onto us or we made a mistake, and our not-so-legal activities would be exposed. We decided to turn the other cheek if another Roland Masters came along, and let it be someone else's responsibility.

We knew how lucky we had been and didn't want to press it any further. In most of my killings, it would have only taken one small thing to go wrong to tip the scales and make me the victim instead of the enforcer. Perhaps the way Roland's situation had developed gave me some clarity about just how fate had been on my side and how precarious that was. Who could say, when Roland came back from the trunk with the hammer in his hand, if he had suddenly recognized me, figured out what was about to go down, and used the hammer on me? If that had happened, it would have not only killed me, but then Stella would be left alone with a hammer-wielding rapist on a dark, very deserted road, in the middle of nowhere. We decided to retire from killing bad guys and let the law enforcement people do their jobs.

I think just making the plan to travel for a few years and starting anew on the road gave us hope for a bright future. Breaking off the ties with the Witness Protection Program was going to take a load off Stella's mind. She never trusted the promised confidentiality.

Keeping out of trouble was going to be a priority. It wouldn't do to have our van searched with all of the guns and ammo stashed in the back. Another good thing was to get away from New England and their ridiculous gun laws. I looked forward to moving on to other places where the right to protect your life and the lives of your loved ones was respected. Many of the places we planned to go would be abundant with wild animals and having a weapon could make the difference between living and dying, eating or starving. One never knows.

There are also unknown dangers from two-legged animals. Both of us had seen "Deliverance." We had four good weapons and a ton of ammo for each of them, plus an assortment of knives, axes and hatchets for the many chores for which they would be needed around a campsite.

We bought a small easel, some painting supplies and a folding stool for Stella, hoping that with the dangerous life finally behind us, she could re-introduce herself to an old passion from another time, which was painting. She asserted that at one time she was quite good, but she needed peace and solitude to get in the zone where she had to be, to flow with the natural beauty she found in painting.

I bought a few fishing supplies, hoping for time at last to relax, drop a line into a lake somewhere and enjoy a little peace and quiet. We also put in a decent collection of paperback books. I had always been an avid reader and was finally going to be able to spend some time enjoying the escape from reality that a good book provides. All in all, with our new attitudes and expectations, we were leaving the park, our work, and all the turmoil we had, behind us. We were pretty excited about this new adventure. All we asked was to be safe from harm and left alone.

Now we were ready to go.

We gave two weeks' notice at work, said our goodbyes to the few friends we had there and tied up all the loose ends we could think of.

Of course, our employer asked us to stay. They didn't know what our plan was and we were leading them far astray from what we were actually going to do, for obvious reasons. A few of our co-workers had seen the van, so they had an inkling that we were going to be doing some camping, but we never let on to what extent. We didn't want to be found.

Our immediate supervisors also begged us to stay, but not knowing what they were up against, they couldn't offer us anything that would change our minds.

Stella contacted her agent at the Witness Protection Program, code named "Slugger," and told him she was going off the grid, out of the Program and would no longer be his responsibility. He was quite upset and tried to talk her out of it, but his was a hard sell, and Stella stood firm.

He asked how she expected to stay out of harm's way. Stella replied that keeping on the move and having no contacts should make it fairly easy.

She did not tell him anything about me.

After a very long time debating the wisdom of what she was planning, he finally wished her the best. He asked how he could get in touch with her, should the heat finally be off. She said he couldn't because we weren't going to be in one place for any long periods of time. He begged her to keep in touch with him and she finally promised she would.

We were finally ready to leave. With any luck at all, it was going to be a very good life.

# 30

There was nowhere in Connecticut we wanted to be, so for the first day, we mapped out a course to drive toward New York, with our first camp-out somewhere in West Virginia. We wanted to find a sparsely populated countryside, where we could easily lose ourselves. We read that the scenery was wonderful there and forests were plentiful, so that, we decided, was our first destination. Fall was approaching and we eventually needed to head south or west to get to a warmer climate for winter, but for now, we wanted a taste of the remote beauty that West Virginia offered.

As we were leaving the park, we almost collided with a dark green Ford recklessly barreling in with a big guy driving and three frightened male passengers. The driver was either late for an important meeting or just in a big hurry, because he wasn't paying any attention to safety. His passengers looked so terrified, it was comical. As he careened by us, kicking up dirt and rocks from the shoulder, we laughed about how good it was to be getting away from the crazy New England drivers. They were always in such a hurry with nowhere to go. It's been said that Florida has the worst drivers in the country but after spending as much time as I had in New England, I thought they might be wrong about that. We weren't going to go to Florida to see.

Our van was equipped with a powerful V8 engine, so it was quite nimble on the highway with plenty of reserve to handle hilly roads.

We knew gas mileage was not going to be the best, but it handled nicely and was very comfortable. The captain's chairs in front felt like recliners. It was large enough to hold the supplies we needed, yet small enough that Stella could maneuver it as easily as me. We had taken out the rear seats and sofa, but the bed we installed and all the supplies we brought more than made up for the weight we removed. The van rode like it was heavy because it was. The roof container stored most of our supplies and fishing and painting equipment as well as our clothes, but didn't make the van top-heavy at all. I considered it all money well spent.

We made our way to I-95 and meandered south through New York City, eventually hooking up with I-76 in Trenton, New Jersey. We followed this into Pennsylvania until we arrived at a small campground near Harrisburg. We slept on the bed in the van that first night because we wanted to get back on the road early in the morning, in hopes we would be in a less traveled area by mid-day the next day. The maps we picked up promised a more rural countryside once we penetrated the interior of West Virginia.

Early the next morning, we turned onto I-81 south, which took us directly into the Appalachian Mountains. This was where we wanted to be. We exited on State Route 250 in Virginia, driving west, and by mid-afternoon we were finally in West Virginia. We were blessed on that first full day on the road with clear, mild weather, not too hot and not too cold. We watched the countryside closely and consulted the wilderness maps and information pamphlets we had purchased, to find a remote place to spend the night.

About fifty miles into the state, we made a sharp right turn onto a two-lane road that was not on the street map, but was on the wilderness map. There were no street signs and there was no neighborhood to identify with if we ever wanted to find it again. It was all mountainous and forested and more different from Lost River than one might think. We were quite taken in by the beauty surrounding us. I stopped the van for a minute to stretch our legs and when I turned off the ignition, we marveled at the quiet. There was an ever-so-slight breeze coming from the north whispering through the trees, but other than that, not a sound was to be heard. We walked around the van a few times, stamped our feet to jumpstart some circulation, and just soaked it up for a minute or two. Then, with eager anticipation, we began the last leg of the day's travel.

By late afternoon, we were well into the Otter Creek Wilderness near the Monogahela National Forest. It was a bowl-shaped valley, formed by Otter Creek, between McGowan Mountain and Shavers Mountain, slightly west of the Shenandoah Mountain Range.

Near the bottom of one valley, there was an opening in the woods on the left side of the road that we thought might hold some promise, so we ventured in to see what we could see. Driving on a grass path which was once a road, I began to think about inadvertently starting a fire from the heat of the catalytic converter beneath the van. The catalytic converter was a smog control component, shaped like a muffler, built into the exhaust system that incinerates any unburned fuel that would otherwise come out of the tail pipe. It burns this off using extreme heat caused by a reaction of the exhaust mixing with chemicals in the converter. This extreme heat could transfer to the surface of the converter and start a fire if it came in contact with high grass or tinder. I couldn't remember for sure when the government began making Detroit install them in trucks, but I thought the van probably had one.

Because I was unsure of its location, I didn't know how high the grass would have to be to touch it. I figured as long as I didn't park in tall grass, it would probably be OK. We didn't want to come into West Virginia for a relaxing, tranquil visit and then burn the state down.

After making our way through about a half mile of ruts, rocks and potholes, the path opened into a good-sized clearing which looked like it would be a safe place to park and camp for the night. We had not seen any "No Trespassing" signs and it had no fences or gates blocking it off. Tomorrow would be a good time to do some exploring and see what the immediate countryside had to offer. We thought the land must belong to somebody, though unlike in the western states, there was no barbed wire keeping people in or out.

The clearing was about a five acre square and had almost no grass. This eased my fears of the van starting a forest fire, so after a short look-around, we decided this would be home for the night.

We had practiced putting up and taking down the tent three times before we left, so getting it set up for the real thing was an easy job, taking only about ten minutes. We erected it at the far edge of the clearing, with the van close by, so our provisions and equipment would be almost beside us. The tent was a green camouflage color and blended well with the woods behind it. It was practically invisible from the other side of the field. The ground was fairly soft, so putting the pegs in to anchor the tent down was accomplished with just a boot sole pushing them in. It had evidently rained recently, making the soil soft, but I wasn't worried about wind pulling up the stakes and blowing the tent away. If that became a concern, we had some extra-long tent stakes in the van which we could use. There was no wind and the sky was clear, indicating there were no storms coming in. I made a mental note to buy a barometer to help with weather predictions.

Besides the small refrigerator, we had two coolers, one of which held some steaks, bacon, pre-made hamburgers packed in ice, along with onions, pickles and a few packaged condiments. The other contained drinking water, sodas, wine and some wine coolers. Of course, we brought gin, rum and vodka for special occasions. We also had an assortment of canned meats for sandwiches. Stella had a small box containing different kinds of seasonings, so supper would be a feast, no matter what we cooked. Neither of us were big beer drinkers, so we hadn't brought any.

Stella and I gathered downed wood to use for a campfire and while I shaved bark and small pieces to use for kindling, Stella made use of my handy old Army entrenching tool to clear off a patch of grass large enough to be sure our campfire wouldn't spread. I placed eight adequate sized rocks, taken from remnants of a wall behind the van, in a small circle, and set a round metal grill from a backyard barbecue on them to cook burgers. The grill would also support the coffee pot in the morning. The shavings were dry and I easily started a fire with one wooden match. Once the fire was going well, Stella put a couple of patties on the grille along with some onion slices and a sprinkle of garlic salt, and cooked some delicious burgers. We sat on the coolers, eating and laughing, enjoying our supper like we were at C J's Burgers of the Great Outdoors.

After we ate, we removed our chairs from the rear doors of the van and moved closer to the fire. I opened the gin and made a couple of drinks. Then we sat back, sipped our drinks and took in a beautiful sunset, well fed and at peace with the world. The sun goes down early when you are in a valley and when darkness came, it fell quickly.

Stella wanted the van close to the tent so she could use the porta-potty without having to walk too far in the dark. She didn't want to have to go into the woods to take care of her needs because of a concern for snakes. I told her not to worry, as they didn't have snakes in West Virginia. I didn't think there was much truth in that and she probably didn't believe me anyway, but I said it to ease her fears as much as possible. The light from the fire wouldn't reach the forest and we only had one flashlight, but I think she would have declined the foreboding of the woods no matter how many flashlights we had. It's funny how something that looks so beautiful in bright daylight can take on such a sinister appearance in the darkness.

I was constantly making mental notes about things we would need if we were staying in one place for any length of time. We needed more than one flashlight, for sure, and I thought I should purchase a couple of folding lounges so we could stretch out like we owned the place while watching the sunsets.

The evening was beautiful, with a gloriously colorful sky to the west, around the setting sun. There were just enough clouds to give us a patchy red sky as the sun said goodbye for another day. We had mountains to the east and south, so we wouldn't see the sunrise in the morning until it came over the mountain, but it was a small price to pay for that beautiful evening view. There was always the possibility that whoever owned this land would come here tomorrow and kick us out anyway, so we were not making any long-term plans for staying.

By the time it was full dark, with only glowing embers left in the fire ring, we were tired from the long day on the road, so we got our bed ready quite early. The surprising tension of leaving, the miles we traveled and the fresh air made us both sleepy. There was nothing to stay up for anyway. We inflated the queen bed air mattress, zipped our sleeping bags together to make one, and we were ready for our first night alone in the boonies. We brought our handguns into the tent, just to be on the safe side. There was no way of guessing how many critters lived in these woods and not knowing how big or bold they might be, we thought we should be better safe than sorry.

We didn't have the rain fly on because of the clear sky, and I opened the moon roof flap at the top of the tent. Lying there, we could see the stars. It was a magnificent sight, much brighter than you see in the city because here in the forest there were no lights from businesses, cars and street lights to reflect into the sky. As we snuggled, Stella quietly murmured, "I think we've finally left it all behind."

I agreed, "It's probably safe to say, at last we're in a position to choose our own destiny." It felt good to be able to say it and really mean it.

Lying there taking in the beauty of the heavens, Stella turned her head, looked at me and asked, "Chris, do you suppose anyone else has what we have?"

I answered, "If they do, they are the third and fourth luckiest people in the world."

We made slow love there in the wilderness, beneath the stars shining into our tent. It was a fitting way to celebrate our new-found freedom and the quiet life we were going to have for as long as we wanted.

I couldn't know just how wrong that prediction was and it's probably a good thing I didn't know. For now, we were grateful for our good fortune. We were so blissful and contented in our bed that a bear could have ripped into the tent and eaten us before we knew what was happening.

# 31

The next morning, because we had gone to bed so early the previous night, we were awake at the crack of dawn. I always wondered how girls named Dawn felt about that analogy. It was an old high school joke, but it still made me laugh every time I heard it. I guess you had to be there.

I started a small fire and put the coffee pot on the grille. It was daylight and as the magic of the wonderful night dissipated, reality became a little clearer. While Stella was in the van, using the facilities and I was in the woods taking care of my needs, I began to ruminate on the things I so far had done wrong. Not knowing where we were, I should have brought the van closer to the tent, for protection as well as masking some of the glow from the campfire, small though it was. I also admonished myself for leaving our long guns in the van when we retired to the tent for the night. I should have known better. When we brought the hand guns into the tent we were thinking about the four-legged animals in the woods that could be frightened off by a gunshot, but forgot about any who wouldn't be frightened by a gunshot. I likewise should have thought to set out a trip wire, which would warn us if anyone approached our camp in the night. Like typical city folks, we forgot about the two-legged animals. Protection from them was just as important as a critter that is probably more afraid of us than we are of them. Stupid city folks.

We decided to explore these woods and find out if there was anything we should know about or be concerned with. After looking around a little, if we were as alone as we thought, we could decide on a plan to stay another night, or two, or three, or to move on. Having spent part of a day and a night there, it seemed peaceful enough, and it was breathtakingly beautiful.

We had provisions for ten days at the very least, so it wasn't like we had to rush off and find a store. Besides, I felt like playing Mountain Man for a little while. Stella was right beside me with a glowing face, anticipating a full day of exploration. In the end, we decided that the safety of our surroundings would be best determined by exploring the territory on this level first. We were both charged up for a day of hiking in the wilderness.

We talked about it over breakfast. We cooked bacon, then eggs in the bacon grease and sopped up the leftover grease with buttered French rolls. It was a delicious breakfast, though we could almost hear our arteries hardening while we ate. It was tasty but extremely unhealthy. We packed up enough supplies to hike as far as we wanted today. We planned to hike toward the south for half of the day, leaving the second half of the day to get back to our camp before nightfall.

There was a small trail going into the woods which appeared to skirt the mountains, so for our maiden adventure, we opted to begin with an easy route. It would give us a better idea how big this beautiful wilderness was, and if there was a farm or something around the other side of the mountain. Who knows, we might find a combine humming or silos hiding defense missiles, surrounded by armed guards and security cameras. There was only one way to find out. If it got too late to get back to our camp in daylight, we would simply sleep under the stars.

We carried small backpacks with a few supplies and wore shoulder holsters in which to carry our handguns. We thought about only bringing handguns, but the more we thought about the unknown, neither of us had any desire to negotiate a right of way with a wild boar, or some other kind of dangerous beast, armed with only a handgun. A wild boar or some other angry animal with razor sharp tusks, hoofs, teeth or horns probably wouldn't willingly make many concessions. It wouldn't do to get ripped open by a predator out here, just as we were embarking on a whole new way of life. So, Stella carried the Ithaca pump 12 gauge shotgun and I brought the AR15. We filled our pockets with ammo for the long guns, plus I had three extra magazines for my Colt, while Stella had three extra clips for the Sig. Considering all we had been through, and carrying enough firepower to hold off Santa Anna's army, it was hard to get too excited about a pig.

We each put a package of beef jerky and five energy bars into our packs and carried full canteens of water. We decided not to bring our bedrolls because we didn't intend to stay in the woods overnight, but we did roll up and attach waterproof ponchos to our belts in case a mountain storm came upon us. We laced up our hiking boots, grabbed binoculars out of the console in the van, strung them around my neck and after locking up, set off walking into the path at the base of the tree line. We followed what looked like a small trail. It may have originally been man made, but it looked like it was strictly a game trail now. From what we saw while skirting the perimeter of the campsite, the surrounding woods had many small trails. We chose this one because it looked like it might lead us to the area we wanted to explore today.

The footing was mostly level and easy for our first day of hiking, with grass not too tall and fallen branches and trees at a minimum. It was very pretty and I was wishing we had brought a camera. We took our time, resting often to look around and listen for any signs of civilization, but all we heard was the quiet of the woods, occasionally broken by a birdcall or a rustle that let us know there were critters here who probably didn't like us disturbing their home.

The forest wasn't terribly dense, though occasionally there were places where you couldn't see far into the trees. Most of the time, you could easily stray from the trail if you weren't paying attention, but it didn't seem dangerous in any way. Being away from city noises was a welcome change. It was a treat not hearing loud mufflers, tires on pavement, screeching voices, trash trucks, pressure release whistles or ambulance sirens, that you get so used to hearing when living in civilization. You don't know how noisy living among people is until there aren't any people and those sounds are not there. You find your ears straining to hear, but there are no sounds other than your footsteps and your own breathing. When we stopped moving it became even quieter.

There were occasional brooks and streams that looked clean enough to drink, but we had forgotten to bring purification tablets, so we weren't going to taste any of it. I made a mental note to be sure to bring them with us on our next exploration.

We hiked the trail around the mountain until almost noon when we found a place to sit and eat. Lunch consisted of beef jerky, an energy bar and a few swigs of water. I made another mental note to bring coffee in the thermos. I was really wishing I had a strong cup right about then. It was nice to rest for a bit, but the lunch was sorely lacking. You learn a lot on your first venture into the woods. Mostly, you learn what you will do differently next time.

So far, we hadn't come across any animals that we could see except for squirrels chattering at their unwelcome guests. We saw no signs of any people. It had been a pleasant hike, not terribly strenuous and one that we really enjoyed, but we decided to head back to camp. It was easy to follow the trail to return, but again, I made a mental note to get a small compass in case on one of our hikes, we wandered from the trail.

The wilderness was a pleasant change from town, but I wouldn't want to be lost in it.

When you are preparing for this kind of new life, you try to think of everything, only to find that once you are in the woods, there are so many things you forgot. Another thing we didn't bring with us was insect repellent. By mid-afternoon, we were being dive bombed by mosquitos and a few other kinds of bothersome bugs and flies. We had purchased four spray cans of repellent, but we then carelessly left them in the van. I guess lessons learned the hard way are best remembered. My mental notes were turning into a small book.

It was surprising how different the woods looked, hiking in the opposite direction, and I wondered if we might have become lost if not for the trail. Not only was a compass an important thing to have, I decided it might be a good idea to leave a marker every so often to guide us on future return hikes. At least for as long as we were still easily confused tenderfeet.

It didn't take as long to return to camp as it had to go that far, perhaps because we weren't stopping as often to look at the beautiful scenery. When we arrived back at the camp, everything was the same as we left it. Our first excursion into the woods taught us things we had not thought about. What stood out the most was that our lunch wasn't nearly hearty enough for the calories we burned. We were famished and our energy levels were way too low. More mental notes.

I started a fire under the grate in the campfire circle and when it was hot enough to have some coals in the bottom, Stella wrapped a couple of potatoes in a double layer of tin foil and stuck them in the coals to bake. They would take a half hour to cook, so when she was finished with the potatoes, she seasoned a couple of small steaks in preparation for supper.

When all was cooked and ready, we took the folding chairs out of the van, used the coolers as a makeshift table, opened a bottle of wine and had a hearty meal.

Sitting there eating, Stella looked around and said, "Isn't it amazing. Here we are, completely removed from society, sitting in the middle of nowhere, eating steaks and drinking wine like civilized people."

I replied, "Society is what you make it. How could life feel any better than it does right now?"

"After all the pressures we had in the past and all the things we've had to deal with, we are as content as two people could be. This is our new civilization."

We agreed that it was hard to compare the pressures and fears under which we had lived to the peace we felt right now.

We finished our supper and tossed the paper plates into the fire, washed up the rest of what we used and concentrated on emptying the bottle of wine. By the time it became dark, the fire was down to just coals and I was wishing we had some marshmallows. Yet another thing for that growing mental list.

By the time it was full dark, we made our way into the tent, exhausted by a full day of hiking and fresh air. Drinking an entire bottle of wine contributed as well, but the important thing was, we were happy and grateful to be away from the world. Stella felt good that the shackles of the Witness Protection Program were finally off. She felt that in killing Fat Boy for murdering her sister, she not only exacted revenge, but ended a potential threat to herself. It was a good feeling.

We had every intention of reading for a while, but while undressing for bed, that old familiar coppery taste rose in my throat and before you knew it we were again in the throes of lovemaking. It was a much better way to end the day than reading a book.

# 32

The next morning, we were once again awake before the chickens. We slept extremely well on our air mattress/sleeping bags bed. We had placed a heavy blanket under the sleeping bag to insulate us from the cool air in the mattress, which worked wonderfully. Many campers don't understand that when you are going to sleep on an air mattress or a cot, you have to put blankets under you, as well as on top of you, or you will be cold. We had slept like the dead. You could attribute that to exhaustion from the trail and all that fresh air, or to the wine, but I felt like it was a release of tension. It seemed like we hadn't been stress-free in a very long time.

After another greasy breakfast, we decided to follow a trail which led north for our second excursion, just to see what was there. Tomorrow we would tackle one of the tougher mountain trails.

For lunch, we brought a can of sandwich chicken and a few bread rolls, four packets of mayonnaise we had stolen from a fast-food joint, a few chocolate chip cookies and a full thermos of hot coffee. Two canteens of water and a package of jerky rounded out our lunch menu. We also made sure to have energy bars in our packs at all times.

Starting off in the opposite direction was strange at first because the sun was in the wrong place in comparison to where it shone on yesterday's journey. It felt like we were coming back to the campsite instead of hiking away from it.

We also brought a spray can of deep woods insect repellent, so we were well prepared for those ornery bastards.

This trail had more brush and rocks, so the going was slower, but twenty minutes into the hike, it began feeling like we were moving ever so slightly downhill. I occasionally left small, but conspicuous rocks on the path, so we would be sure to find our way back. It's easy to get directions mixed up in the forest, especially if it became stormy or dark, so we thought leaving a trail to follow was a good move.

The downhill walk wasn't a sharp drop, but barely perceptible though it was, it was definitely downhill. An hour later the trail leveled off and the woods opened up to reveal a small pond which was probably made from mountain runoffs similar to the streams we saw yesterday on the other side. The scenery was beautiful, as it sometimes is when near water. You have the beauty of the scene itself, plus what is mirrored off the pond.

Stella stopped at one spot and said she thought this would be a beautiful scene to paint. It sounded like a plan to me because we could come here for a day or two so she could paint and I could fish. I could almost taste fresh mountain trout cooked over a fire. We stayed there for half an hour and then continued on.

Except for the pond we found, there wasn't much else of importance, so we took a break for lunch, made sandwiches from the canned meat we brought, ate all the cookies, drank the coffee and started back toward camp.

The hike back was slower because the almost imperceptible downhill slope on the trip into the woods became a definitely noticeable climb on the way back. It wasn't terribly steep but it was constant, so our legs felt rubbery soon into the return hike.

When we got to the pond we had admired on the way out, it was even prettier from this perspective. There were many scenes for Stella to paint and there was plenty of bank area, with and without shade, from which I could fish. It looked like this hike turned into a win-win. There was something here for both of us to enjoy.

After taking another twenty minute break, we continued back to camp. Because we brought insect repellent, of course there were no bugs today. Someone must have told them we were armed and ready for them.

We arrived back at camp earlier than the day before, probably because we hiked a shorter distance and didn't stop as often. It was time to try out the shower rig.

I pulled it out and quickly set it up. It was framed with pliable white fiberglass rods, which made it free- standing over the rubber pad I brought for just that purpose. It had a curtain that hooked on the top rod and wrapped around the entire thing. It covered you down to about ten inches off the ground, surprisingly affording pretty decent privacy.

Then I connected a shower hose with two ends on the back side and a small sprinkler head on the end that you used. One hook-up went to the cold water pump and the other, to the hot water heater. It had a simple mixture valve for adjusting the water mixture to a comfortable temperature. I took off my clothes first, stepped in and gave it a whirl. When I turned the water nozzle on, it was at first cold enough to take my breath away. After adjusting the mixture, it warmed up quickly. I wet myself down, shut off the water flow, soaped up and then rinsed off. It worked much better than I thought it would. I had forgotten to bring shaving equipment, so my mental list grew longer. Besides, Mountain Men don't shave, do they?

When I was done, Stella shucked her clothes, jumped in and did the same. It felt good to be clean and smelling like civilized people out here in the middle of nowhere.

Once we were done with bathing and personal hygiene, it was time for supper, so we cooked some burgers, washed them down with wine and settled in for the night.

We were very pleased with ourselves and how things had gone in our first two days and nights in the wilderness.

The only additional thing we needed to do was incorporate vegetables into our diet. While beef was good, and we knew from finding the pond that we would soon have fresh fish, our bodies would require greens and fruits to stay healthy. More things to add to the mental notes.

We got to bed early and actually did open a couple of books to read while we snuggled, but soon our eyelids wouldn't cooperate.

The night was chilly, but we were as warm as we wanted to be in the tent. It was tightly sewn, so it did a good job of keeping the wind out and the warmth in.

Soon it would be another dawning.

# 33

fter another very unhealthy breakfast, we decided to hike up the mountain this day before exploring any more of the level trails. We knew it would be more exhausting, but we thought we would perhaps have a better understanding of our surroundings if we could see the area from a higher vantage point. So far, our base camp was turning out to be a very nice place to stay. I looked forward to catching some fish out of the pond we discovered and adding some diversity to our diet.

Unhealthy or not, we knew the breakfast would provide the energy we would need for an active day. We placed some leftover bacon in a baggie along with buttered biscuits and canned roast beef sandwich meat for a more hearty lunch. We also brought beef jerky, a half dozen energy bars and just for the heck of it, a can of sardines. We filled two canteens with water and brought another one with orange soda in it for the sugar content. This would assure us of a good lunch.

We didn't want a lack of energy to create a problem, especially on the uphill climb. I once again brought coffee in the thermos. The caffeine had given us a boost yesterday, but I guess that's why we drink coffee. It certainly isn't for the taste.

We put our small backpacks on, making sure we had the flashlight, insect spray, extra instant coffee packets, sugar cubes and two butane lighters. I also tied a small bag containing a collapsible coffee pot and collapsible cups to the outside of my pack, which I had picked up at the camping store in Hartford. I didn't know how well they worked, but guessed we would find out. We packed extra ammo for our weapons into ammo pouches that clipped to our belts and hooked our bedrolls and groundsheets on the back of our utility belts. The bedrolls and groundsheets were very light, so their weight wouldn't bog us down. Except for the two canteens of water and one of soda, the ammo was the heaviest thing we were carrying, but we felt that next to food and water, ammunition was probably the most important thing to bring. It wouldn't do to run into a band of perverted mountain dwellers and not have the firepower to defend ourselves. The food and water weight would obviously lessen as we ate and drank.

I once again grabbed my binoculars and we started up the new trail.

There were many switchbacks up the side of the mountain, which made the trek longer, but it was easier than trying to climb straight up the side. It was much slower hiking than yesterday, and we stopped and rested more often, so we knew we weren't going to cover nearly as much distance as we did hiking on the flat trail. I also took the opportunity to form two walking sticks from branches of a fallen tree which were the perfect sizes for us, to aid in the uphill climb.

We continued to marvel at the beauty and solitude of the woods and found it amazing how quiet a wooded area can be during the day, despite the present, but unseen animal population. It was warm, but not hot, and there was no breeze, which brought out an occasional swarm of gnats. Getting closer to fall, there were not as many as there could have been, but they were still a nuisance. It wasn't long before we sprayed each other with the insect repellant, quite happy we remembered to bring it. It was much better not having to deal with the aggravation of flies and gnats. They still buzzed around our heads, but they weren't landing, so it wasn't terribly irritating.

We zigzagged for a couple of hours before we came to a level area with a small round clearing, no more than 80 feet in diameter. It had a gentle stream running through it and soft, green grass blanketing the ground. We had again forgotten to bring water purification tablets, so I underlined my mental note for our next hike. As alluring as the cold water from the stream looked, there was no way to judge the bacteria level in it. There could be a dead animal lying in it a hundred yards upstream, or perhaps a hillbilly washing his feet. Even with purification tablets, I would be reluctant to drink it without boiling it first, unless I absolutely had to. I wondered how many hikes into the forest we would need before we remembered to bring everything. It was turning out to be quite a learning experience. Relaxing at a campsite or in your home on a sofa in a warm, dry living room, you think you can plan to cover all the bases, but once you get out into the wilderness, you find out how much you didn't think of. It's pretty humbling.

We took a break at the oasis, appreciating the stillness, and split an energy bar, washing it down with water from a canteen. Then, shouldering our packs, such as they were, we continued up the trail.

The hike up the mountain was every bit as beautiful as the trails we covered the previous two days. Every time we thought we had just seen an amazing sight, there was another scenic view to stop and admire. Years of living in the city or the towns we were familiar with makes you forget all the beauty nature offers. At the same time, we were reminded that we weren't on a smoothly paved road or path. The going was rough, often with trees across the trail and occasional places where rainfall had washed part of the dirt away, but the inconvenience of these things was a small sacrifice for the time we were having.

By early afternoon, we decided we were most likely going to stay on the mountain for the night, so we broke for lunch, making sandwiches with the canned beef and biscuits, and sharing some of the soda. After taking a half hour to let our food digest, we ate another energy bar and drank coffee from the thermos. More than anything, we were taking a breather. We weren't in any hurry. Having hiked up this mountain for the better part of the day, we found no reason not to spend the night up here and return to our base camp in the morning. We didn't want to have to try finding our way back in the dark, for fear of getting lost. Stella led the way up the trail for another hour until we came upon another clearing of sorts, high enough to give us a good vantage point from which to look around. I took out my binoculars and we climbed a huge, flat rock which overshadowed where we were going to camp for the night. We took turns looking in every direction and saw no signs of life to the east, south or north, pretty much confirming that we were truly alone in this wilderness.

When I peered through the binoculars to the west, after scouring the area a bit, I found the clearing where our base camp was and after a short search, clearly saw the van. It seemed so out of place and unnatural there in the wilderness.

Looking further beyond it, I could see where the road entered the clearing, as much as there was to be seen, and thought how lucky we were to have found it. We tried to guess, as the crow flies, how far we actually were from base camp, but it was a hard thing to do with any accuracy. If we were crows, it was probably only a couple of miles, but it was considerably longer hiking all the switchbacks of the trail on two legs.

At dusk we made a small campfire, ate another energy bar and the can of sardines, washed them down with water and called it supper. Energy bars and the rest of the bacon and coffee made from the instant packets we brought would have to be breakfast, but we didn't mind at all. We were having a heck of a time.

The adventure of the forest was worth the small inconveniences and we probably wouldn't be hiking up here again, so we concentrated on making the best of a not-so-bad situation.

We had hiked quite a distance in the last three days and as far as we could tell, we were completely alone. These excursions eased our minds about staying at our base camp for a few more nights or perhaps longer, before looking for another paradise.

Not having a tent for shelter, we gathered downed pine boughs to serve as an adequate mattress for the night and put down our ground sheets and our bedrolls. When darkness descended, we snuggled to each other with our weapons at our sides and went to sleep. We were too tired for lovemaking that night, but it was a good tired.

As quiet as the woods seemed during the day, it was noisy as hell at night. Because we were not making any noise ourselves to drown out the natural sounds of the forest, the night sounds were amplified. In the darkness, it sounded like a thousand critters were scurrying about, taking care of their nocturnal chores.

It wasn't that much of a bother, other than the noise at first disturbing my sleep, but I could tell Stella was tense. God forbid one of those critters should unwittingly bump into either of us in the middle of the night. We would probably empty an entire magazine wildly into the forest, only to find out it was a harmless chipmunk.

The sounds made our imaginations think there were mountain lions thundering down on us or a band of Bigfoot primates preparing to have us for a midnight snack. With the fire completely out, in total darkness, your mind can produce a host of improbable scenarios to frighten you.

# 34

Waking just after first light, we enjoyed lying there, listening to the morning sounds of the forest and marveling at just how quiet it was compared to the sounds of the night. I'm sure it was just as noisy as it was in the dark, but being able to see there are no mountain lions or monsters attacking you quiets one's imagination. I made another mental note to pick up a lightweight two-man pup tent for any similar excursions in the future. If it had rained during the night, we would have been soaked. We hadn't thought to bring a hatchet to cut branches to make a shelter.

When the darkness was completely gone, we rolled out, stretched, and wandered off just far enough to discretely heed the calls of nature. Then we ate the rest of the cold bacon and biscuits, topping breakfast off with another energy bar. We thought about a fire to make coffee but decided it might be better when part-way back down the trail.

Stella asked, "How long do you think it will take to get back to our camp?"

I replied that we would most likely be there before noon. It would be much quicker going downhill. She was already speaking of the camp as home, displaying her natural nesting instincts. Compared to where we had just spent the night, the camp would seem like the Hilton. We had slept some, but the pine boughs weren't very comfortable.

I got up, removed the lens covers from the binoculars and looked once again in an attempt to determine how far we were from our base camp. At first, when I zoomed in, it looked the same as when we saw it last, the only difference being the light coming from another direction. After a minute of scouring the location, I observed a man in dark clothes, standing just to the side of our camp, peering into the hillsides with binoculars. At first, I thought he must be a hunter, but looking closer, I could see he wasn't wearing hunting clothes. Then I thought he might be the farmer who owned the property, looking to see who was trespassing on his land. But he wasn't wearing farmer's clothes either. It looked more like he was wearing dark gray work clothes. He looked very much out of place. The man appeared more like a city slicker who was out of his element than a local, so the next question was, what was he doing out here in the forest? I couldn't shake the feeling that there was something funny looking about his clothes. They weren't the clothes of a woodsman.

As I looked longer, a sudden pang of warning hit in the pit of my stomach. Behind him, just inside the edge of the clearing was a dark green Ford sedan, parked almost out of sight. I remembered seeing a green Ford tearing into the trailer park just a few days ago as we were leaving. Then I saw another man come up and say something to the guy with the binoculars. If he answered, I couldn't tell from this distance. There were some animated gestures between them, so I supposed they were having a conversation. One was more animated and vocal than the other.

A closer look revealed that they weren't wearing gray city clothes at all. They were wearing dark gray or black, one-piece coveralls, the kind you would expect someone to wear over street clothes which they could remove and throw away when they finished whatever it was that dirtied them.

Foolishly afraid of them hearing me from this distance, I quietly called Stella over, told her what I saw and let her look through the binoculars. The color drained from her face when she saw them.

She asked, "Who the fuck is that?"

I replied, "I don't know, but they're obviously looking for something. Or someone."

The more I watched, the more it dawned on me that instead of looking for something, they were looking for someone. And the only people out here were Stella and me.

I asked Stella if she remembered the green four-door Ford speeding into the trailer park when we were leaving. As she continued to look, she said she did and agreed that it looked to her like the same green car.

I recalled there were four guys in the car, so that must mean there were more people we couldn't see.

I took the binoculars again and looked as closely as I could, hoping to see a shiny badge or something resembling a law enforcement logo, but I couldn't see anything like that. These guys weren't cops.

If they were the same people we saw careening recklessly into the trailer park, it could only mean they were looking for us. This was no coincidence. Had we just been lucky to be leaving at the same time they were coming in to find us? And why would they be looking for us? If they had found us at the trailer park, what would they have done? They were definitely not cops, so they weren't here to arrest us. That only left one other thing. If they weren't here to arrest us, they must be here to kill us. That would explain the coveralls.

This was a Wet Team.

Assassins.

I shared my suspicions with Stella, trying to understand what was happening. Were these guys here to seek revenge for someone I or we killed? Roland? Fat Boy? Kevin? Mr. Farmer? Beaver Shit? I left virtually no trail in any of these killings and if I had, I would have been caught much sooner than this.

Something was fucked up here.

As I played everything through my mind I had to conclude that except for being an accessory in Fat Boy's killing, none of the worthless people I killed had any connections to someone who would send pros out to get me. That left Stella.

I knew she had taken out a few assholes before she met me, but neither of us had gone into all the details about the who or the where in our previous lives. It would have been like describing time with past lovers. There are some things you don't discuss. It was time to put our heads together to try to see who was fucking with our lives now. These guys were sent by somebody who wanted us dead. It must be something from Stella's past because I couldn't think of any reason someone would send heat like this after me. The closest thing I had negligently done was leave a drippy faucet in the mobile home when I sold it. Hardly a hanging offense.

I expressed my thoughts to Stella and could see that her mind was racing through her experiences too.

Finally she said, "I think it has to have something to do with Fat Boy George. I set him up, knowing he was the guy who killed my sister. I also knew he was going to take the money himself and kill me because I am the only witness who could tell his boss that he was stealing from them. The way it went down, it seemed like he was acting alone. If George told someone else, why didn't they come with him? If there was an accomplice, I probably wouldn't have been able to kill him. Was this about the guy who came to my apartment? Is this who these guys are? Are they more assassins?"

We had no way to know. All we could see was the obvious, that someone was looking for us. And I didn't think it was to bring our Publisher's Clearinghouse winnings.

We had never gone into specifics about just how much of the mob's money her father had lost. Stella revealed it was around a half million dollars with interest. At least that's what they tried to squeeze out of Stella and her sister. That would explain them killing Patty and why they threatened to kill Stella if she didn't give up her father. It's pure fiction out of an old movie that the mob doesn't go after families.

Stella thought that by investigating what went down with her father, stalking the guy who killed her sister and finally setting up the sting that killed him, the heat would be off. We both thought Fat Boy was working alone, but if he was, who are these guys and where did they come from?

# 35

By this time Stella was almost in tears. I would have tried to console her, but I needed to hear more of her story so we could figure a way out of this mess.

I asked what else happened that we hadn't talked about and what about a guy who came to her apartment. Stella wiped her eyes and filled me in, "After George killed my sister, before I went into the witness protection program, I started carrying the Beretta that I took from the bank robbers because I knew the FBI couldn't stop the mob from killing me. They would only investigate after the fact and fill out the correct paperwork when I was dead. They talked to me about the protection program, but I wasn't sold on the idea yet. I lived in a second floor apartment and one night I heard a noise on the fire escape outside my window."

"I knew there was someone coming for me. I secured my Beretta and hid behind the drapes by the window he would be coming in, with the gun in my hand. I was no sooner hidden when a man came in the window like a thug from a Humphrey Bogart movie, carrying a small revolver and wearing a black ski mask. When he was fully through the window, I stuck the Beretta behind his ear and told him to drop his gun and to put his hands on his head."

"Hearing a woman's voice, he relaxed, thinking his time would come soon, so for now he complied. I backed away, pointing my gun at his head, made him get on his knees and take off his mask. He was a very small, scary looking man with a shock of red hair and a scar next to his right eye, which had been badly repaired. It looked like a drunk blind man had done the stitching. I made him take off his belt, lie on his stomach and put his hands behind him."

"I used the belt to bind his wrists. It's not like I was experienced at this, but I was doing whatever I could think of to neutralize the threat. Nobody else was protecting me, so I was on my own. I was in shock because even though they had killed Patty, I never thought this would really happen to me. I guess I was living in denial."

She continued, "This guy had found me, but I needed to make sure he wouldn't be able to tell anybody. I knew right away I couldn't let him go. I think he knew it too, but I also thought he kept expecting to get an opening which would give him the upper hand. I made him go into my bathroom and climb into the bathtub. Once he was in the tub, I questioned him about who sent him and why. He wasn't being too cooperative, so I used a bathrobe belt hanging on the back of the door to tie his feet so he couldn't kick me and told him I wanted answers and I wanted them now. Once again, he thought a woman wouldn't be ruthless, so he wasn't talking."

"I opened my makeup drawer and located my cuticle knife. It's not big, but it is razor sharp and it looks like a little scalpel, so it immediately got his attention. I slit a hole in his pants and poked his scrotum with the tip of the knife. I asked him if he would rather I cut his balls off before or after I killed him. I told him either way, if he didn't tell me what I wanted to know, I would cut them off and feed them to the first stray dog I found."

By now, Stella was rambling with the story, so I let her continue, "I asked if he had an accomplice, which he denied. I asked why I should believe him and he said I could look out the window and see his car at the bottom of the fire escape with no one in it. He said he left it there in order to make a faster getaway."

"With a little coaxing and an occasional poke, he became nervously talkative. He told me how much money my father owed and when I asked again who sent him, he said it was a man named Tommy Bolser. He admitted he worked for the Organization, but couldn't tell me how far up the ladder this Bolser guy was. It wasn't a name I was familiar with. Bolser wasn't a name I heard in the information I received which led to me tracking down George."

"Then he got apologetic and told me that he was forced to come after me because if he didn't follow orders, they would kill him. He would not give me his own name, but assured me that if I let him go, he would never bother me again. I asked what he was ordered to do to me and he went silent because he knew I wasn't stupid."

"I told him I was putting the towel in his mouth until I decided what to do with him. After I gagged him and told him we couldn't stay here, I picked up my gun, stuck it against his chest and shot him where I thought his heart would be. I must have been right because he died immediately. By holding the gun against his chest, the shot was muffled and really not loud at all. I knew none of the other tenants would report it, because it was just one small noise and wasn't repeated. Not an unusual happening in an apartment building"

I was spellbound. I knew Stella was much tougher than she looked and that the tender side of her could change quickly. I also knew I didn't blame her for killing this guy. Under the circumstances, she didn't have much choice.

I asked, "What did you do with his body?"

She said, "I put on a pair of dishwashing gloves and dug out a new shower curtain, while leaving him in the tub to bleed out so he didn't make a mess. His heart must have stopped pumping immediately because there wasn't much blood at all. I brought in a small throw rug from my living room, pulled him out of the tub onto the shower curtain, rolled him and the curtain in the rug and tied the ends up with a couple pieces of clothesline."

"I waited until about two in the morning, dragged him to the window and slid the rug with his body in it down the fire escape. My biggest fear was the rope breaking, but it didn't. It was only from the second floor, and it wasn't as hard as it sounds because he was pretty small and not heavy at all. Once we were on the ground, I dragged him into the backseat of the car in the alley. He only weighed about a hundred pounds, so dragging the rug was easy, and his car was right under the fire escape, so I didn't have to drag him far. It only took a few minutes. Thankfully his keys were in the ignition. I dreaded the thought of having to un-wrap him to look for them. I drove about a mile from my apartment, wiped down everything I had touched, locked the car up and walked home."

"In the morning, I called Slugger, my contact for the Federal Protection Program, and told him I wanted to go into the program immediately."

# 36

S o now the entire story was out. It was a safe bet these guys in our camp were not here to arrest us nor were they even looking for me. They were here to kill Stella and I would just be collateral damage. Despite Stella killing two people they sent for her, they weren't giving up. The question remained, how did they find us? Before we left Lost River, we told very few people where we were going. We hoped these assassins hadn't hurt any of our friends to get information on our whereabouts. Even if they did, we had not given anyone details or specifics about where we were going.

Except Slugger, Stella's Witness Protection contact.

She remembered how, when she contacted him to tell him she was going off the grid for a while, she may have given him a few details about our plans. The assassins must have gotten to him just before we left. Perhaps they threatened his family or something. That would explain the Ford barreling into the mobile home park as we were leaving. Missing us by a margin that narrow was fortunate for us, and it must have really pissed them off.

The entire time Stella was in the program, her biggest fear was an information leak. Evidently, her worst fears were realized.

The cold hard fact was they were here to kill us. The leak in the system would have to go on the back burner for now. If we got out of this, we would decide then how that would affect our future. The leak wasn't the immediate problem. If we weren't successful with these yahoos, it wouldn't matter, because we would be dead.

The only way out for us was to kill these guys before they killed us. Killing more people wasn't a pleasant thought. It was something we never wanted to do again, but at least we knew where we stood.

The first thing we had to do was to think like them. We were here in the woods, a little out of our element, but the assassins, if there were still four of them, were more than a little out of their element. In these woods, they stood out like turds in a punch bowl. They were probably city boys, which I thought was an advantage for us. They were used to cornering their prey in an alley somewhere, beating or killing them, and going home to a sofa, a few beers and TV afterward. I doubted they were accustomed to slogging around in the woods in West Virginia.

We had to put ourselves in their shoes, anticipate their plans, and be a step ahead of them. We knew they wouldn't leave any witnesses. Likewise, we couldn't leave witnesses. The sooner we understood that, the clearer the picture would be. A tall order, for sure, but we couldn't allow any of these thugs to get away and bring reinforcements.

Four against two gave them a big leg up, but there was still the outside chance that there were only the two we had seen. I wasn't banking on that. Likewise, who was to say there were only four? For all we knew, there could be another car parked behind the Ford, out of sight, with a half dozen more assassins. We couldn't afford to take anything for granted or even think about best case scenarios. We needed to anticipate the worst.

Trying to figure who had what advantage, we knew the numbers were in their favor, but they also probably figured Stella, being a woman, would be a pushover. To think that would be a big mistake. Soft and beautiful she might be, but she could be as hard as stone if it came to our survival. She had proven that to me as well as a couple other people who would never be able to talk about it. If they had seen Fat Boy's head, they wouldn't think Stella was a pushover. That car trunk looked like someone exploded a bag of Jello in it.

They thought they had the element of surprise, not knowing we spotted them in our campsite. That turned it around and made it an advantage for us, so we hoped to be able to use that element of surprise on them. These guys probably thought they would just hunt down and kill a couple of tenderfoot, weekend campers, unable to protect themselves. This was another checkmark in our column.

We had another advantage because the trail wasn't new to us while it would be to them. We had these few things to work with on top of which, we were carrying a ton of ammo, so we weren't going to run out of firepower any time soon. We would shoot until either we got them or they got us, and we had a little bit of time to plan how, while they found their way up the trail.

Stella asked, "If they look, they will see three different paths we took, so how will they know which one to follow?"

I pointed out, "Because two of them have tracks going and returning. The tracks for the mountain trail only show our tracks leaving. This will be the one they follow, because they will know we haven't returned."

We hoped they would be sloppy because they didn't think we knew they were here. They were also probably used to winning. In their business, if you don't win, you're dead and they were still alive. When you win all the time, you sometimes forget to consider that you might lose.

Another advantage for us was that they were probably cocky while we were scared, and frightened people can be like cornered animals. Everyone knows cornered animals are dangerous. We had to be the cornered animals.

They were most likely heeled with just handguns, probably nine-millimeter semi-automatics or .357 magnum revolvers. They would be surprised to know we had two powerful handguns, a shotgun and a high powered rifle. They probably thought we were just two kids out on a hike with not much more than a walking stick and a pocket knife.

Underestimating our firepower could be a big mistake for them. If they had any suspicions that we were armed as well as we were, it might give them pause. At most, they likely thought we had .22 rifles or some such, which would give them a lot of confidence. They probably didn't understand how fast confidence can get you killed.

They would see the trail head as well as we did and maybe better, because we had trampled into it the way we did. Following our tracks shouldn't be too hard. We hadn't known there was another human within miles of us, let alone killers on our trail, so we never would have thought to erase our tracks.

Trying to guess how far these assassins were behind us was tricky. I didn't think they would start up the trail in the dark, so we should gauge their time on tracking us by how much light there was. It was barely light when I spotted them this morning with the binoculars, so assuming they started hiking up the trail somewhere near that time, they would still be hours getting to us.

The two we saw might not be the ones coming for us, but perhaps rear guards staying in our camp in case we returned from another direction. Considering all factors except how many there were, which was only a guess, we thought they wouldn't reach us until mid-day at the earliest.

We didn't know what kind of shape the climbers were in, so judging their speed would be a guess too. We also couldn't know how they would handle thin air from the elevation or whether they were carrying provisions or water. From what I saw, there didn't appear to be any packs or other preparation for a prolonged hike in the forest. They probably thought this would be a quick hunt-down and kill. An easy days work.

We guessed they would beat our time by one to two hours because they weren't carrying any weight to bog them down and they wouldn't be stopping to admire the scenery.

That still left us plenty of time to be afraid.

We went to work formulating a plan for an ambush. They wouldn't know if we were still climbing the trail or on our way back down, which should create some indecision. They didn't know we were aware of them on our trail or that they were intending to kill us, so they would not be thinking they could be ambushed.

They were most likely expecting to find us dumb and happy, coming back down the trail without a care in the world. We should be easy pickings.

All of these advantages I thought we had could be wrong just as easy as right and that would spell disaster. We needed to be right.

The only sensible thing I could think of was to go up the mountain a little higher and leave evidence of our passing, so they would have to climb higher to find us. This would add to their fatigue factor.

I didn't think these guys were athletes, so they would be tiring quickly. The fact that they had no food or water or anything to prepare them for spending a night in the woods should make their tempers short when they didn't find us right away for a quick kill. This was another small advantage.

We could only hope they drank stream water along the way.

I reasoned that after we made them tired and a long way from our camp where their backup people were, we should go off the trail where we couldn't be seen, and double back. If we could, we should find an ambush spot from which to take them out on their way up the trail. If that didn't work out, we could try to ambush them on their way back down after they lost our trail. A lot would depend on how good our ambush site was if we could even find a suitable one. We would deal with whoever was back at the camp later, assuming there was a later. These two, three or four thugs would have to be our priority for now. If there were more than four, the outlook could be bleak, but right now, we couldn't think about that.

We headed gingerly up the trail, hiked for about two hours, and jumped off the trail at a bare spot of rocks so they could not see where we left it. We made the assumption that none of them were trackers, so it would look like we disappeared into thin air.

The going was much harder for us coming back down because we were off the trail. There were trees down everywhere and in places we had to take detours because of roots and branches growing in a tangled mesh so thick that it would take a machete to cut through. We were taking far too long to get back to where we wanted to set up our ambush.

In about three hours, we finally came to an area of huge rocks that I thought stretched back as far as the trail. It would be a perfect site to catch them in a cross-fire. I saw a similar rock cropping on the trail when hiking up and thought these might be an extension of what we saw now. We had to be as quiet as possible too. Because we had taken so long, there was no way to tell how far away our stalkers were.

It turned out these rocks were indeed part of where I wanted to make a stand, but we had veered much farther off the trail than we thought. We were grossly behind where we wanted to be by this time.

My only reservation was that if I was the hunter, I would be wary of being tricked, and I would be afraid of these rocks. Anyone who ever has read a western book or seen a western movie would recognize this as a good place for an ambush. But then, these guys were goons and goons don't read or have much for brains, so I calmed my fears ever so slightly with that theory.

So far our luck held up, but taking longer to reach the place for our ambush, we didn't know whether we were still ahead of them or behind them. We decided to hunker down and wait. Time would tell.

Stella set up behind some rocks on one side of the trail and I inspected my field of fire from the other. We didn't know if we would be shooting uphill or down the trail.

We ate the last of our energy bars, not knowing how long it would be before we ate again. Mostly we watched and listened. The forest was brimming with the activity of birds calling to each other, with a moderate breeze blowing leaves and bending whatever grass there was. The wind kept the bugs down too, so that was a plus. We didn't want our stalkers finding us because they smelled our insect repellent.

Taking up positions across from each other would put them at a disadvantage because we would be shooting at an angle that might take them a second to recognize, and a second's advantage might be enough. Throw in a little luck and we just might see the sun rise tomorrow.

The trail was narrow enough that they would be walking in single file and we had talked about me shooting the first man and Stella shooting the second.

After that, for however many there were, it would be a free-for-all. There wasn't much cover for them, so we were hoping to get off second or third shots if we could before any of them made it to the shelter of the rocks. If anyone made it to shelter, the ambush would be less effective because their cover would then be equal to ours and the element of surprise would be compromised.

So, we waited and waited, keeping in each other's view, expecting them to come huffing and puffing by at any minute. I had no reservations about Stella being a good partner for this operation. She was as lovely as a woman could be, but when it came to a situation where our lives were at stake, she would be a good back-up. My fear was that I could be taken out once we opened the dance, leaving Stella to fend for herself. I knew she would fight like Davy Crockett at the Alamo, but we all know what happened to him.

It was now getting to be late afternoon and there was still no sign of them. We began to doubt our prediction of their arrival. Had they started up the trail earlier than dawn? Were they simply fat, out of shape martini drinkers who were only able to climb at a snail's pace or were they already beyond our ambush site?

By the time dusk was less than an hour away, we knew we had miscalculated. It couldn't be taking them this long to get this far. They must have passed us somewhere while we were making our way down on the other side, off the trail. We were so far off the trail that evidently we never heard them and they never heard us. It was time to regroup and implement Plan B.

The catch was, we really didn't have a Plan B.

I moved across the trail to Stella, so we could discuss the situation. We agreed they must be further along. This meant nothing as far as when they started up the trail and perhaps guessing about that had thrown us off. It just meant that they made good time climbing up the mountain and we had made very poor time coming back the way we had. Our bruised shins from tripping over unseen rocks and logs, and scratches from occasional surprise branches in the face were proof of that.

We guessed that the hunters wouldn't find where we skipped off the trail before dark and assumed they had no light to see by, so it was as safe as any other assumption we made today that they wouldn't be coming back down tonight. There was about an hour of daylight left, so we decided to go further down the trail and try to find a better ambush spot to use when they came down in the morning.

We started down the trail, looking for just the right place and found it after only about twenty minutes. It was a far better place for picking someone off who was coming down the mountain. There were more woods than rocks, giving us a better choice of where to place ourselves where we would have the best field of fire. We were sure they wouldn't come down in the dark, so we made ready to spend the night.

Ours was a good hiding place, with high rocks behind us and breaks here and there in the rocks in front of us filled in by wooded sections. We laid out our ground sheets and bedrolls and prepared to wait. We were both exhausted from the off-trail hiking and not having enough food, but the tension from the whole situation was the most strength-sapping thing of all. We knew we were only one small mistake away from dying tomorrow and yet, despite the mistakes we made today and the miscalculation of the killers' time on the trail, we were still breathing. The problem was, so were they.

Even knowing they wouldn't come down the mountain during the night, we prepared ourselves to be on alert in case they did, so I told Stella to get some sleep while I kept watch. When I got sleepy

I would wake her up so she could watch and listen while I got some rest. It turned out, as tired as we were, neither of us slept anyway. There was too much at stake to let our guard down even a little bit until this was over.

# 37

Long before there was enough light to see, I was already searching the trail with the binoculars for any sign that they were on their way back down. We were out of food and had just a little water left, but we knew they were worse off than we were. I had seen no evidence that they had any supplies at all, which meant they spent the night being eaten by bugs, with no food or water and most likely no sleep.

Our stalkers were probably hungry, thirsty and not just a little bit cranky. They hadn't found us, so they must think they suffered a miserable night in the woods for nothing. Losing our tracks and having to come back down empty handed must have them riled. Goons are used to success and don't deal well with failure. They must be thinking we came back down another way, which meant their whole excursion including the discomfort was a waste of time. For all they knew, we might have come down another way, killed their lookout and made good our escape. They were as cut off as we were and my bet was they didn't like it.

Hearing and seeing nothing, I ventured out to look for berries or anything else that might be edible, but had no luck at all. When I returned to our hideout, Stella was calm, knowing that this was going to be the showdown day. She was a most amazing woman. She knew what had to be done and now she was ready to do it. It took nothing away from her feminism, but I had to wonder where she got her nerve. She was determined to walk out of here. I wished my resolve outweighed my skepticism. All we could do was give it our best and hope that once again, good would triumph over evil.

It was closing in on noon when we heard them clomping down the trail. Maybe they thought we got away, because they were throwing caution to the wind. They made more noise than a refrigerator falling down three flights of stairs. It sounded like all they had on their minds was getting out of these unfriendly woods and back to civilization. I didn't think they had any intention of staying the night out here, sleeping on the ground with no food or water. I doubted they had a very nice night.

They must have thought there was no threat because they made no effort to conceal their presence. We heard them for a full five minutes before we saw them. Sound carries a long way in the forest.

There were three of them. They were arguing about what could have become of us and how we couldn't have simply disappeared. One guy was adamant in telling the other two that there must be another trail that we took which bypassed them.

Because of their bickering, we now knew there was only one guy left at the camp. His name was "Bill" and they hoped he was able to get us before we got clean away. The loudest guy didn't sound too hopeful, so we wondered if Bill was the most inept of the four and that was why they left him as the last bastion of defense. When we were finally able to spot them coming through the forest, we could see one pretty big guy leading, followed by two smaller, but not really small guys, in single file.

They were trying to hurry, which was difficult because although there was a trail, it was small and there was considerable debris to trip over and swear at. They obviously thought we were gone, but one of the smaller men observed the stand of trees, shrubs and rocks where we were hiding on opposite sides of the trail. He turned to the big guy, who was evidently the leader, and said, "Hey, look at that place over there! We should have just waited for them yesterday right in those rocks and ambushed them on their way down!"

The big guy answered with disgust in his voice, "They came down another way, you dumb bastard! Otherwise we would have seen some sign. All you want to do is sit on your ass and hope they come by, but they ain't gonna, so shut the fuck up!"

The other smaller guy agreed and spoke to the big man, "You know, it's a good thing you remembered seeing that van coming out of the trailer park. If you hadn't, we wouldn't have known what to look for."

I was glad to hear that because now we could be sure they were the ones recklessly speeding into the mobile home park. All doubt was removed that we had to kill them.

All of them.

I looked longingly at Stella and she returned my gaze. It was like a silent just-in-case good-bye, for we knew the showdown was going to happen in the next minute.

Last night when we couldn't sleep, we talked about what to do if one of us didn't make it. Of course, if neither of us did, it wouldn't matter. Stella and I were realistic enough to know the odds weren't with us. We knew what banks our money was in, knew account numbers and where we had money stashed in safety deposit boxes. If one of us was killed, the other wasn't to wait, but get out of there and go away as far and as fast as we could. It didn't make for a nice discussion, but it was important that we understood what the survivor would do in a worst case scenario.

I made a motion to Stella depicting a fat guy, confirming that I would take out the big guy, and one of the other guys would be her first target. They were lumbering down the trail in single file, with the big guy in front, so Stella held up two fingers indicating that she would take the second guy. We could then both gang up on the third guy. We were confident in our abilities with these weapons, and we hoped to get clean kills with our first shots, before they knew what hit them. We didn't have time to have to fire twice at the same target.

That would just expose us to whoever was left alive. If we both missed our first shots, we were as good as dead anyway.

We were close enough for Stella's shotgun to do a terrible job on flesh and bone if she pointed it right. My tumbling AR15 load would blow a hole through the big guy and take out a slew of vital organs with it, but we had to be on target the first time. The third guy might pose a problem, if he was quick. He could get off a couple of shots that could hit one or both of us.

They were, as we suspected, only carrying handguns, but they were close enough for a good chance of accuracy and they were already carrying them in their hands. They might be goons, but goons usually know how to shoot. Carrying their guns in their hands make them quicker in getting off a shot than if they had to reach for a holster. This was going to be chancy, but we had no choice. A lot was riding on our success.

We had already unlimbered our long guns, and we both had handguns if needed, so we were fine in that sense. We had only one chance to find the range.

I got the big guy in my scope, wishing I had taken it off the gun. He was so close, I could shoot better without it. I looked at Stella and held up five fingers. She nodded and I started the count, five, four, three…. Then the clock in our heads took over as I sighted the big guy in again. When the count got to one, I let out a breath and gently squeezed the trigger. Stella fired at the exact moment and our targets collapsed like someone pulled a big plug and let the air out of them.

The third guy got off a couple of quick shots, firing wildly in my direction and Stella's. His shots at me were scary close, careening off the rocks behind me. This guy could shoot! I couldn't see if his shots in Stella's direction were close or not. I quickly looked for a thumbs-up from her, but she was not there.

I couldn't see her, so I knew at least one of his shots must have hit her. I moved to my left so the same thing wouldn't happen to me. This wasn't going as planned. Despite all of the talking we did about the possibility of one or both of us dying today, I was still stunned by the reality that Stella was down.

I knew the grief would hit me later, but right now I didn't have time for it. I was in a fight for my life and couldn't afford to think. I got off a shot in the last guy's direction but missed. By now, he had found a hiding place behind a big tree that might have been an oak, but I couldn't identify it. I didn't know much about trees. I did know I couldn't see him and I didn't know if he could see me.

For a few moments, all was quiet. The respite didn't serve me well because it gave me that moment to think about Stella, and I didn't want to think about her right now. I had finally found the girl of my dreams and just like that, I lost her. The thought was too much to bear.

I looked again where Stella had been hiding, but she wasn't there. I peered around more and there she was, circling to her right. When she had moved about fifteen feet, she took a shot at the third guy. Her slug hit the tree hiding him, and took a chunk out of it, missing him by bare inches. He quickly turned away from that side to line up return fire toward Stella, momentarily exposing himself to me. I put a bullet in him before he could take his shot.

I dropped my rifle where I stood, pulled out my Colt and ran out of the rocks to make sure they were all dead. My first shot, a clean center mass shot had killed the big man instantly. There was an exit hole in his back the size of a mailbox. Stella's shot at the second man had gone high. Instead of a center mass shot, he didn't have much left of his face. These goons would kill no more.

While I checked the first two, Stella ran over to the third guy behind the tree, with the 9mm in her hand. Evidently, he wasn't dead because she put a slug into his head, closing his case.

The relief that Stella was not hurt was indescribable. When she came over to her first victim, I expected her to be repulsed when she saw what was left of his face after being hit by her shotgun blast, but she wasn't. She looked at him with satisfaction in the set of her jaw.

After a long, thankful hug that we were still alive, we looked at each other with the same thought.

Three down, one to go.

# 38

I didn't want to stop hugging Stella, but we had to plan how to handle the remaining soldier. We knew there was only one because we had heard the big guy speaking sarcastically about him. That told us that maybe he wasn't as good as these guys were. Surprisingly, these guys hadn't turned out to be very good. They made about every mistake you could make in the woods when stalking someone you are trying to kill. For mob guys they had not been professionals. A professional comes prepared, uses every precaution, and never, ever lets his guard down. The dumbest hiker could have killed these buffoons. They gave up too soon, wrongly made the assumption that we were gone, became loud and careless, and it cost them their lives. It raised speculation about whether these three were the best of the four or the flunkies.

Was the guy left at our camp, in fact, the leader and competent one?

No longer in a place where we could see the camp through binoculars, we could only guess what he was doing. The fourth guy would have been instructed to wait there no matter what. I knew from my experiences in combat, that the human psyche is not patient and only the best trained soldier can wait forever. My bet was that hearing the shots probably made him skittish and it would not be long before his patience ran thin.

If he wasn't as competent as the three we killed, he probably didn't have much for planning skills. The rub was, there was always the chance that we could be wrong. If he was actually the leader, perhaps he sent in the flunkies to rout us out of the forest, so he could pick us off like ducks at a carnival. He might be tougher to kill than we hoped.

We decided to move a little further down the trail and try to find another ambush spot. In contrast to how the other ambush turned out, we planned to shoot him on his first pass up the trail. If he got by us and saw what we did to his partners, it might make him careful enough to avoid us entirely. Letting him find a way out could bring reinforcements and we would be in bigger trouble than we were now. If we could get him on his way up the trail, shooting at him from slightly different angles at the same time, he wouldn't have a Chinaman's chance.

After about fifteen minutes, we found a spot that was going to have to do. It was only a clump of trees, but he wouldn't be able to see us from the trail, so we decided to settle in there and wait, on opposite sides of the trail.

In about an hour, knowing darkness was only a little while off, I wondered if he was going to come up looking for his buddies or if he had jumped in the Ford and took off when he heard all the gunfire. He wouldn't know at first whether the gunfire meant his partners won or lost. When his accomplices didn't return, he would know. Hopefully he was coming in to help and not running to get help.

It would be too dangerous to take the fight to him. To go down to our camp to see if he was there would be a huge risk because we had no idea where he was. It was much more spread out than the thick woods and there would be a hundred places to hide. Two of us couldn't possibly cover every angle. If he was sharp at all, he could pick us off easily once we cleared the trailhead. All he would have to do is find a place to hide, aim at the trailhead and shoot us as soon as we broke out of the cover of the woods. He probably didn't know we knew he was there, so in his mind, killing us should be easy. He would be counting on us thinking we were safe.

So we were back in a waiting game. Would he come up looking for his friends or would he sit back and wait for us? It was clearly his choice to make. We weren't going anywhere.

After a while, I changed my position to get a better look at the trail, and climbed up on a small rock. Just as I did, I felt a terrible pain in my right leg and simultaneously heard the boom of a shot as I was knocked to the ground. The sharpness of the pain was excruciating and I couldn't move my leg. The pain was quickly replaced by numbness in the entire leg. Now I was unable to feel it at all. Being thrown to the ground confused me and made me temporarily disoriented. The son of a bitch had taken a page out of my book and hiked up parallel to the trail, so Stella and I were looking in the wrong direction!

It took a few minutes to realize I wasn't mortally wounded, but I didn't know if I could move. I decided my best bet was to stay down and not give him another shot. I didn't know exactly where he had fired from or where he moved to after he fired the shot. He clearly must have been the smartest of the four.

He called out, "Annie, you can't get away! I just killed your boyfriend so he can't help you! Why don't you come out, give yourself up and see if we can work something out. I'm sure you can convince me to be nice to you! It will be like one hand washing the other, right?" Then he cackled like the pervert he was.

I oddly wondered, "Do all the mob guys rape their victims?"

Stella didn't answer and there were a few minutes of silence.

He called out again, "Annie, you had better think about being nice to me because if you don't come out I'm gonna get mad. And if I get mad, I'll make things more fun for me, but it won't be fun for you!"

By this time, I figured Stella would be pretty frightened, thinking I was dead. She was out here all alone, pinned down by this shitbum, who wasn't making any bones about his intentions. He was assuredly going to rape her, probably in ways she didn't want to think about, and there was no escape. She must be thinking that our past finally caught up with us. What a lousy way for it to end.

I didn't want her to think she was alone, but I couldn't call out because it would not only let Bill know I was still alive, he would know where I was. In our current predicament, that wouldn't do.

I decided that as bad as I might be hurt, I couldn't just lay there and let this happen. We weren't going to die like dogs. If this motherfucker was going to kill me, I was going to die fighting.

I raised myself up on my elbows so I could see beyond the rock that I had fallen from when he shot me and there was Bill, as big as life. I lifted my AR15, sighted in on him, pulled the trigger and heard a click. The fucking rifle didn't fire! It had evidently smashed on the rock as I fell and sustained damage so it wouldn't fire.

My movement and the sound I made drew his attention. When he saw me, he turned, raised his pistol and said, "Gun won't shoot, huh? Too bad, asshole."

Then there was a blast that took him off his feet. Stella came rushing out of the brush with a look of determination on her face, her pistol in her hand. She stood over him and said, "Yeah, too bad, asshole."

Then she shot him six times in the chest. As Stella's bullets went through him, they took big chunks of his lungs and other tissue with them.

All stuff this guy wouldn't need anymore.

She ran to me with genuine concern on her face and asked me where I had been shot, feeling me all over, looking for an entrance wound and not finding one. It seemed Bill's lack of pistol expertise was his demise. His shot had taken off the heel of my boot. He must have aimed low, expecting the shot to go high, but instead, his shot was true. It had knocked my leg from under me and the impact of the bullet, along with landing unceremoniously on my leg when I fell probably accounted for the numbness.

We looked at each other and started to laugh. We sat there for ten minutes laughing until the tears came down our faces. It may seem like a silly thing to be doing after having just killed four men, but that's what we did.

Then, I looked at her questioningly and said, "Annie?"

She replied, "That's a long story. I'll tell you about it with a drink in my hand, and a cigarette in my mouth, basking in the glow I'll be in after getting my brains screwed out."

There was nothing I could say to top that. I think she had a deal.

# 39

We left the corpses in the forest, thinking that if and when they were found and identified, being mob guys, the authorities wouldn't spend too much time worrying about what happened. We hoped the mob would decide their losses were mounting too fast and give up looking for Stella. We allowed that the bodies would probably be eaten by the critters living in these woods and never be found anyway. There wasn't much we could do about the Ford.

By the time we got to base camp, it was already dark and it had just begun to lightly rain. We quickly packed up camp, loaded everything in the van and made sure there was nothing left to show we had ever been there. Once the van was packed, we left right away.

We thought we would drive as far as we could, though we knew exhaustion would take its toll and we wouldn't get far. We were confident we could find a place to pull over and sleep the night in the van. Rain would wash away our fingerprints, footprints and tire tracks, so after we were packed up, we drove around the Ford, out to the street, and got the hell out of there.

We drove about fifty miles until we found a parking lot behind a big, closed retail store. I drove the van all the way to the back of the lot and parked it behind a broken-down cargo truck. We thought adrenaline would keep us awake, but our bodies dumped it fast. We were asleep in five minutes.

I woke up the next morning with Stella's head on my chest. After a few minutes she stirred, looked at me and whispered, "Hello sleepyhead!"

It took a bit to place where we were and what had taken place. When it did, I looked back at her, stroked her hair and said, "You know, I'll bet Flagstaff is pretty at this time of year!"

Ted Taber grew up in a small New England town. He and his wife
Sandy reside in Anaheim, California
    The Killer In Us is his first novel.